## THE BEAST AND THE *bird*
# BURN

# SARAH BALE

**Copyright © 2022 by Sarah Bale**

All rights reserved. No part of this publication may be reproduced, distributed, or transmitted in any form or by any means, including photocopying, recording, or other electronic or mechanical methods, without the prior written permission of the publisher, except in the case of brief quotations embodied in reviews and certain other noncommercial uses permitted by copyright law.

This book is a work of fiction. Names, characters, places, and incidents either are products of the author's imagination or are used fictitiously. Any resemblance to actual persons, living or dead, events, or locales is entirely coincidental.

Cover design by: Sly Fox Cover Design

Edited by: Katrina Harris

Map Design: Brittany Matsen

First Printing: September 2022

Burn: The Beast and the Bird / Sarah Bale -- 1st ed

*To everyone who thought the Beast was cuter than the Prince.
And to those who liked Gaston, even though he was a jerk. <3*

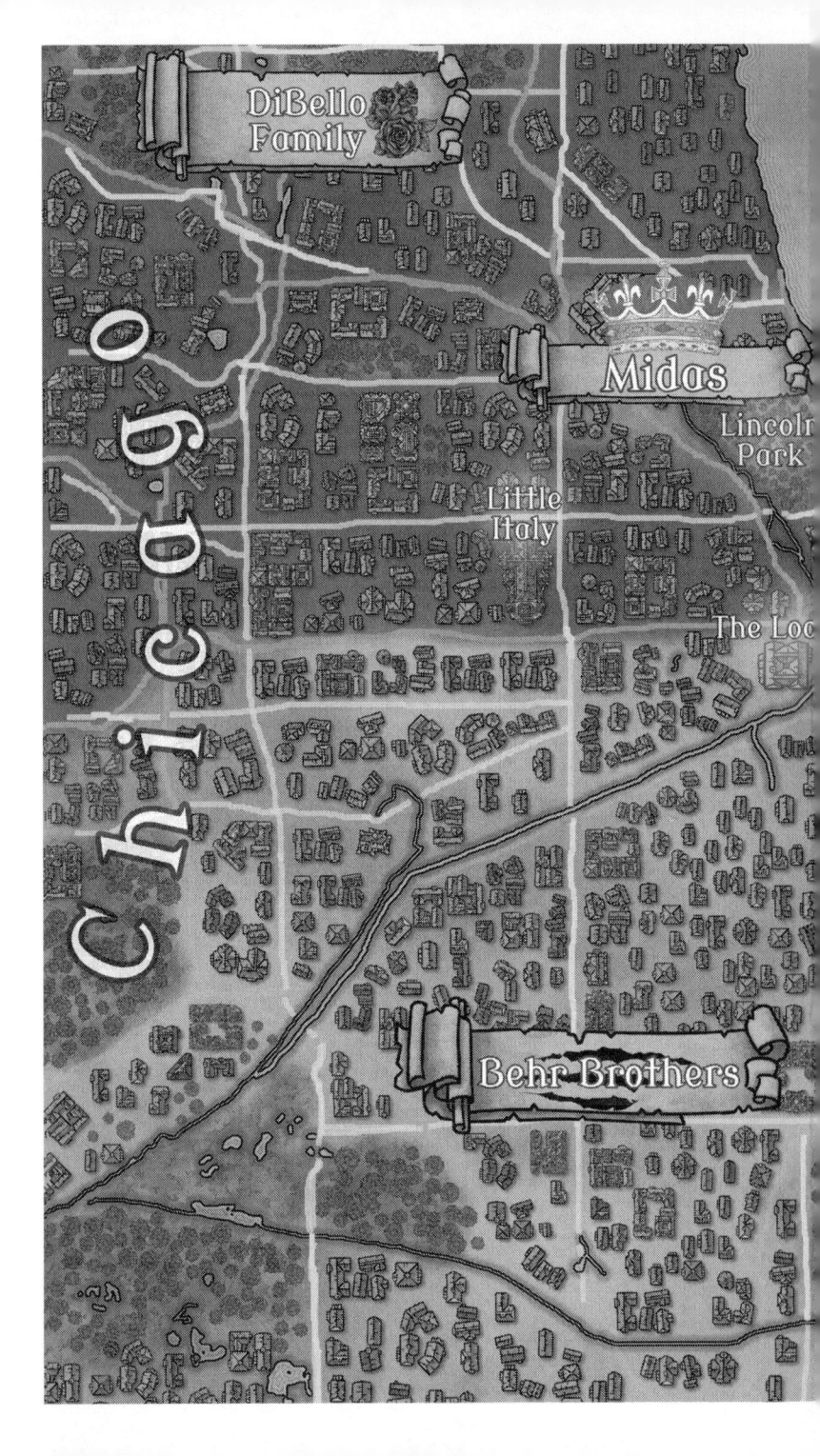

Hook & Co.

## BEAST

I'm the man who always wins.
My prize? Her.
She brings out the beast in me.
She thinks she can outrun us.
She can't.
My men and I will do everything to catch her,
Break her,
Tame her.

## DOVE

My father is determined to ruin us,
Selling me to pay his debts.
I'm not going to sit by,
So I take my siblings and run,
To escape this provincial life.
Too bad they like to chase.

Our passion leads to pain,
Pleasure leads to peril,
And the biggest one of all,
They're going to make me BURN,
In body, mind, and heart.

## CONTENT WARNING:

This book contains situations that readers may find offensive or triggering, including primal kink, mentions of child abuse, physical assault, forced captivity, and other sensitive topics.

Reader discretion is advised.

# 1

*DiBello*

*Dove*

"Dove, where's Dad?"

I turn, holding the wooden spoon that I'm stirring the soup with, and answer my little brother. "I don't know, buddy. I'm sure he'll be home soon."

The lie rolls right off my tongue. If my father is home by Monday, I'll be shocked. It's Friday, which means he's taking his measly paycheck right to the casino or bar. Never mind that I told him I had a date tonight, or that I needed time to study for an exam on Monday. I stir the soup faster, taking out my frustrations on the vegetables in the pot.

"He was supposed to take me to practice. Coach said if I'm late again..."

I bite back a sigh. It's not Chip's fault that our father is an inconsiderate asshole. And god knows I know what it feels like to have people look down on you because of who your father is.

"Let me dress the baby, and then I'll take you."

Our little sister, Belle, has been sick and I hate to take

her out in the cool night air, especially since she just went down. But the hopeful look in Chip's eyes sends me into action. I turn off the stove, moving the soup to a cool burner, and then go into the room that I share with my two younger half-siblings. Belle is sleeping, and her cheeks are rosy with fever. She cries when I lift her from the crib, and I hold her close.

"I know, baby. I know."

Belle looks just like her mother, who left the day she was born. Her hair is brown and so are her eyes, a darker version of my own hair and eyes. Chip has brown hair and eyes, too. Guess our dad has a type. Belle's mother was looking for a safe place to stay and didn't count on my father preying upon her. The thought makes me sick, but I know the truth. I saw it with my own two eyes. She was young and went to the shelter that my dad works at as a janitor, but that didn't stop my creep of a father. When she found out she was pregnant, she moved from the shelter into our house. I tried to be her friend, but she had already shut down at that point. When the nurse told me she was gone hours after having Belle, I wasn't surprised.

Chip's mother died when he was two, but he doesn't remember her. I do. She was mean and liked to talk with her fists. Everyone is better off without her, even if Chip gets sad when he asks why he doesn't have a mom. But he's only six, so I try to tell him things about her that make him smile. Even if most of the stories are lies. He shouldn't have to carry the weight of the person she was. Lord knows our father is going to make it hard enough for him when he gets older.

My own mother is a mystery. My dad likes to say that they were in love, but I find that hard to believe. He said the last he heard that she was alive, but that was years ago. She's never tried to find me in my twenty-two years on this earth, so she must not be that great of a person. In fact, sometimes I tell others she's dead, just to avoid the looks of pity. It used to hurt when I was younger, but now she's just another name on a long list of people who have let me down over the years.

Chip pulls me from my thoughts when he bumps into the door with his bag. "I'm ready."

"Grab the diaper bag and meet me at the door."

I don't dare send him outside. Not in the neighborhood that we live in. There's a literal brothel a few blocks over. It must be pretty popular, though, because there's always a line of people waiting to get in. I've seen some women—sex workers, I guess—at a nearby diner. They always seem happy as they laugh and joke with each other after their shifts, but it's not something I want to expose my brother to.

Belle is still crying as I put her in a warm onesie and load her into her carrier. She settles a bit when I tuck a fuzzy blanket around her. By the time I reach the door, she's fast asleep again. It must be nice to be six months old, without a care in the world.

"Let's go, buddy."

After making sure the door is locked, I climb down four flights of stairs and only have to step over one man who's passed out of the steps. Chip laughs at him, saying he looks like our dad. He's not wrong.

Outside, the air is cool. Even though it's only October, I feel like winter will be here before we know it, and I'm not looking forward to it for so many reasons. Mainly because my income barely covers the bills. The added cost of heating the apartment means I'll have to take a second job on top of the one I already have. Plus college. Plus the kids. It's a lot.

Our saving grace is the help that dad gets from the state for being a low-income household.

*More like no income*, I think bitterly. I can't remember the last time he actually handed over his paycheck to help with things around the house.

I buckle the kids and climb into the driver's seat. When I turn the key, nothing happens.

"Shit."

"You said a bad word, Dove."

"Sorry, bud. The car won't stop. Looks like we're going to have to take the train."

"Yay. I love the train."

I calculate how much money I have. If we take the train to his practice, then I can pay for an Uber to take us home. I hate to waste money like that, but by the time we leave the gym, it will be late, and I don't enjoy taking the kids on the train at night. A shiver works its way up my spine as I remember the last time I rode the train late at night. Two men stood at the front, and I swear it felt like they were watching me. They both had tattoos on the top of their hands. I looked it up later. They were members of the Di Bello Family, and everyone knows the Mafia is bad news.

Lifting Belle's carrier, I say, "Come on."

Chip chatters as we walk three blocks to the train station. By the time we reach the platform, my arms ache from holding the carrier and diaper bag. I should look into one of those baby slings that I see people wearing. I bet Belle would like it, too, since she likes being held. Chip asks for my phone while we wait, so I hand it to him. I should text my boyfriend, Kyle, and let him know that I'm probably going to be late for our date. The thought has me frowning, because I already know he's going to be mad, and I just don't have it in me to fight with him. Not about this, when there isn't anything I can do to change the situation.

Instead, I watch Chip. He plays a game while I shift Belle's carrier from hand to hand. Thankfully, the train is right on time.

"Come on, Dove!" Chip calls out as he rushes into the train car.

The train is busy, and we have to stand. There's a man in front of me with his briefcase in the seat next to him. He doesn't offer to move it, and I don't ask him. Why bother? He'll say no, and it will only piss me off.

We reach our stop and make our way from the train, down the stairs to the street.

"Hey bud, I need my phone."

Chip's face pales. "I don't have it. I think I left it on the train. I'm sorry, Dove."

His big brown eyes fill with tears. Even though I want to be upset that he lost my phone, I can't be. Unlike my father, I realize that words can affect someone for a long time. Am I upset about the lost phone? Sure. Do I realize that it's not Chip's fault since he's only six? Also, yes. Phones can be replaced. My brother's childhood memories can't.

"Don't worry. I needed a new one, anyway. Come on."

He takes my hand, his guilt over the phone already forgotten, and we make our way down the crowded streets to the gym where he plays basketball. As soon as we step foot in the building, he takes off running to where his friends are. Thankfully, we're on time, but I don't miss his coach scowling our way. I get it. I really do. We're *that* family. The ones that make this inner-city team look trashy. And I hate it.

Finding a spot on the bleachers away from everyone, I lift Belle's blanket to check on her. She's still sleeping, and

I'm relieved that her forehead is cool to the touch. One less thing to worry about. Opening my bag, I pull out my math book and notes. It's embarrassing to be taking beginners algebra at my age. There are literal high school students in my class who are taking it so they can get ahead before they actually start college. I wonder what that would be like. To be ahead for once in my life.

When I was in high school, I was an excellent student, despite my home life. But then Chip was born when I was sixteen, and I had to help take care of him. I didn't mind because he's my brother and I love him. But once I got behind, I couldn't catch up. I ended up dropping out and got my GED. Even now, I can only take a few classes here and there. One day it will add up, and I can get a degree. I still don't know what I want to be, but I know I need an education or else I'll end up like my father. And I refuse to let that happen.

Belle stirs, and I rock her carrier with my foot. It's amazing that she can sleep with all the noise in the gym, but she does. Chip is decent at basketball. Well, as decent as a six-year-old can be. He's having fun, which is the important part.

I make a note at the top of my notebook of things I need to do over the weekend. Our neighbor, Mrs. McCarthy, watches the kids while I work. Hopefully she won't mind if I run to the store after my shift tomorrow, so I can get a new phone. Belle needs diapers, and we're going to need groceries soon, too. I tap my pen on the paper, when suddenly I feel that I'm being watched. Glancing around, I see nothing out of the ordinary. I've had the feeling on and off for weeks now, and it's driving me crazy. Strike that. It makes me want to run and hide. But, like always, there isn't anyone there.

I make awkward eye contact with one dad sitting a few rows over. Ugh. I hope he doesn't take this as an invitation to come over and chat. Unfortunately, he does.

"Hey there. Haven't seen you around before. Which one is yours?"

"Number 14."

"Mine are 6 and 7." He holds out his hand. "I'm Doug, by the way."

"Look, Doug, I mean this in the nicest way, but I'm not interested."

"Hey now, don't be like that. I'm just being polite by talking to someone who looks like they could use a friend."

"I'm not being *like* anything. I'm trying to study while my brother plays basketball."

To prove my point, I lift my textbook. His eyes widen when he sees it, and he holds up his hand.

"Sorry. Didn't know you were in high school. It's so hard to tell ages these days with the way you girls do up your make-up."

"One, I'm not wearing make-up. Two, you're proving my point that you're a creeper."

He scowls and stomps off. Good riddance.

I turn my attention to Belle and murmur, "Don't worry, sis. I'll teach you how to tell men off when you're older."

The thought makes me smile because it's actually comical. Sure, I told off that jerk, but I've never found the courage to tell off my own father. Mostly because I know what will happen. My father is anything if not predicable. Drunk. Check. Child abuser. Check. Gaslighter. Check. Asshole. Check. If I ever told him off, it would end with me covered in bruises that I can't explain. Case in point, if I were to roll up the sleeve of my shirt, there would be a bruise in the shape of a handprint around my wrist. So, I've become a master of disguise, wearing long shirts and baggy clothes.

I'm jolted from my thoughts when my very sweaty brother sits next to me on the bleachers.

"Dove, can I go to Beckham's house tonight?"

Beckham is his best friend that he met when the school year started. Each day I get to hear Beckham-this Beckham-that. Mostly, I'm glad he's able to make friends. I was always too shy.

"I don't know, buddy. You don't even have any clothes to change in to."

"I do! I put some in my bag. Please?"

Beckham's mom stands a few feet away, smiling. "We would love to have him spend the night. Beckham has been asking for a few weeks now."

I glance at Chip, who is literally begging with his hands clasped in front of him. "I guess that would be fine."

She reaches into her purse, pulling out a card. "This has my number. Just call tomorrow before you come and get him. And no rush."

The card stock is thick, and probably cost a lot more than I'd be able to spend if I had a business card. I tuck it into my notebook, careful not to bend it.

"Thanks. I have to work until two tomorrow. If that's too late, my neighbor can probably pick him up."

"Two is perfect. No rush at all, really." She turns to the kids. "Come on, boys. We're going to get pizza on the way home."

Both boys run around in circles, yelling, "Pizza!"

Beckham's mom leads them away, smiling. She is a brave woman, because those boys are going to be wound up all night long. I reach for my phone, only to remember that Chip lost it. Well, crap. Looks like Belle and I are going to have to take the train home. It'll be cheaper, I tell myself. That doesn't do much to shake the lingering feeling of dread that seems to hang around me like a blanket.

Lifting the carrier, I make my way outside. It's dark out, and I speed walk to the train stop, thankful there are a handful of people waiting. Most will get off before my stop, I'm sure of it, but at least I won't be alone. When the train arrives, I manage to find two seats, and put Belle's carrier in one. Unlike the asshole from before, if someone gets on and needs the chair, I will move her so they can sit.

There's an intoxicated man at the front of the train car, who is singing loudly. Judging by the puddle on the ground that's moving our way, he's urinated himself. Ugh. Never a dull moment.

"Hey you! You! The pretty lady with the baby," he calls out. "I had a dream about you. They were out to get you, and there was nothing you could do to stop it. So, you better run before the big, bad men grab you."

Goosebumps lift on my skin, and I have to fight physically shivering. Someone tells the man to shut up, and he rants at them. I know he has no idea what he's talking about, but his words have unnerved me. A lot. Largely in part because I keep getting the feeling that someone *is* watching me. *Stalking me. Hunting me...*

Turning my attention out the window, I drown out all the noise around me as the train flies through the night. By the time we reach my stop, Belle and I are the only ones getting off. The drunk man is still there and gives me a smile as I step off the train. I hurriedly make my way down the stairs to the street level, only to find that the streetlamp next to the station is out.

It's only nine, but it feels later with no light. Holding Belle's carrier as close to my body as I can, I head in the apartment's direction. With each moment that passes, I feel that same sense of fear washing over me I've felt for weeks now.

*Run*, my body screams.

Sometimes I can fight the feeling. Tonight, I can't. I pick up my pace. My chest feels tight as I speed-walk down the sidewalk. The hairs on the back of my neck stand, making me terrified to see what's behind me. I shouldn't look, but I have to. Glancing over my shoulder, I don't see a damn thing, but the feeling is still there. There's a black SUV parked on the side of the street. Is someone in there? Is that where this feeling is coming from?

The feeling increases and I face forward. I'm jogging fighting the wind and Belle's carrier. My lungs burn, but I will not stop. I can't. If I do, something bad is going to happen. My instincts scream for me to run, and I'm so close to giving in. My gut tells me that if I run, someone is going to chase. Just the thought makes my throat tight, and I have to fight for my next breath.

If I had my phone, I would call my boyfriend, Kyle. He would calm me down, telling me how stupid I'm being right now. Kyle. Shit! He's probably wondering where I am since I was supposed to swing by his place tonight. Now my pace is hurried so that I can get home and use the landline at our house to call him.

Belle whimpers. God, please don't let her wake up. That's all I need right now, on top of everything else. The intense feeling that I'm being stalked is still there, but now I have other things to distract me. Or, so I think, until the SUV that was parked behind me slowly creeps past. I stumble, almost falling, before righting myself. My apartment building is just ahead, and so what do I do?

I run.

*Luca*

I watch her from the shadows of my SUV as she struggles against the wind and the carrier. She knows I'm here, which makes watching her that much more... *delicious*. It would be so easy to pull up to the curb and offer her a ride. She wouldn't take it, though. I've seen how she acts when males get too close. She's like a spooked animal that needs to be shown what a gentle touch feels like. Or to be brought to heel. My cock throbs at the thought.

The siblings are going to be a problem. She's not going to want to leave them behind, but I'm not looking to have children underfoot. Something tells me I'm going to have to solve this dilemma before I put my plan into action. Wonder how Maurice feels about kids. The thought makes my lips twitch. I can barely pull him out of his laboratory to take care of business. I'm sure a kid would send all the loose cogs in his head spinning out of control.

But something will have to be done, and soon. I've watched her to the point of becoming obsessed. Now it's time to claim her. Dove Potts is mine.

She just doesn't know it yet.

## 2

*Dove*

I hate Mondays, but especially today. My weekend was shit. Belle's fever got so high on Friday night that I had to take her to the emergency room. They gave me crap, since I'm not her parent, and my father was nowhere to be found. But she got the treatment that she needed. That didn't mean she felt much better, though. By the time we got back to the apartment, and I called my boyfriend, he was pissed at me and hung up on me.

On Saturday, I left Belle with Mrs. McCarthy and went to work at the diner. It was busy, and we were short-staffed. To make matters worse, people weren't tipping very well. Half-way through my shift, I got a call from Mrs. McCarthy, saying Belle wouldn't stop crying and that she needed me to come and get her. So, I left work early, and my boss threatened to fire me. His threats are empty, though, because I'm the only person desperate enough to stick around.

When I left, I went to pick up Chip from his friend's house. They live in a high-rise in an apartment that I can only dream about. I felt like trash standing there in my clothes that smelled like fried foods while Beckham's mom chatted with me. Even on a Saturday morning, she was dressed perfectly. Her make-up was even done. Chip was upset that he had to leave so early and begged to stay. Apparently, Beckham has the gaming system that he wants, and they wanted to play a game. Beckham's mom said it was okay, but I stood firm, telling Chip that he still had chores. As we made our way home, he told me he hated me. I know he didn't mean the words, but they still stung. A lot. So much that I cried about it later when I was alone.

Belle basically cried all day Saturday and into Sunday, so no one got much sleep. I had to call in to work on Sunday, since I didn't have anyone to watch the kids. Chip and I were sitting at the table working on our homework when our father finally showed up. He was drunk and reeked of booze, smoke, and body odor.

When he stomped into the kitchen, demanding dinner, he bumped into the table, knocking over the glass of juice that Chip had, and it spilled all over my notes and homework. To add insult to injury, my father grabbed my arm, twisting until I thought he was going to snap the bone, and told me he was sick of me leaving his home in such a state. I cleaned up the mess and grabbed my notes, carrying them to my room. My only saving grace is that Belle was feeling better by that point.

I didn't sleep well, though. I never sleep well when our father is there. By the time my alarm went off this morning, I already had the kids dressed and dropped them off at Mrs. McCarthy's house before making my way outside. For the first time since Friday, I feel lighter, but that does nothing for the dull throbbing behind my eyes from stress and lack of sleep. And, I never made it to the grocery store, so I'm going to have to do that after class. I bite back a groan. I only have one class today, and it's my math class, but that is enough to make my stomach cramp on top of everything else that I'm feeling.

I take the train to the Garfield station, and then hop onto the bus headed toward the university. Many people on the bus are headed to the campus, too. Some even wear UChicago shirts. I should get one to show my school spirit, but they're expensive and I can't justify the extra money. Besides, I don't need a shirt. I need that piece of paper stating I got my degree at the University of Chicago.

A stop before the campus, I hop off the bus and run into a store selling cell phones. It's not as nice as my old one, but it will do. As I leave the store, I turn on the new phone. There's only one missed text message from Kyle, and I laugh. Guess if I ever go missing, no one will look for me. That's not true. Mrs. McCarthy would eventually wonder where I was, but only because of the kids.

Tucking my phone into my bag, I catch the next bus and go to the campus. The drop-off is on the opposite side of the grounds, but I don't mind the walk. I won't feel the same way once snow covers the ground, but that's still a few months off. Okay, at least one month if we're lucky. As a kid, I loved winter. As an adult, not so much.

When I was younger, I used to dream about moving away from Chicago. Back then, it was to go on a quest to find my mother. Now, I know that even if I left, I wouldn't find her. And there's no way I can leave Chip or Belle, so I'm stuck. That's why getting my degree is so important. Once I do that, I can get a decent job, get custody of the kids, and never have to see my piece of shit father again.

But that's going to take time.

What a depressing thought to have. I usually try to

pump myself up before my math class, but looks like that will not happen today.

"On your left," someone behind me calls out.

I move over, so the bicyclist can pass. Every time someone calls that out, I laugh because it reminds me of my favorite Marvel movie. If only Chris Evans could be the one passing me. *That* would make things interesting and get my mind off my shitty life. Instead, it's a fellow student who pedals like his life depends on it. Maybe it does. Some professors are strict and will lock their doors so tardy students can't enter.

I glance over my shoulder again, just to make sure the bicyclist was alone. Once I accidentally stepped in front of a girl on a bike and she crashed hard after swerving to avoid me, and I don't want that to happen again. A man walks several yards behind me, dressed in black jeans and a black hoodie that's pulled over his head. That shouldn't be enough to freak me out because many people around here dress like that, but I can't deny the shiver that creeps up my spine. I can't tell if he's on his phone, but he's definitely looking at me. My breath hitches, and I pick up my pace.

This is the first time I've felt like someone was watching me during the day. It's got to be an overactive imagination, right? I mean, there's no way someone would follow be in broad daylight. But the man's speed is increasing, too. I'm close to one of the buildings, so I dart inside and run up a flight of stairs. Thank god I know my way around, because it's easy to get lost if you don't know where you're going. As I reach the next flight of stairs, I hear loud footsteps. Shit. I think he's following me!

I side-step into the lab, closing the door behind me. Sure enough, the man rushes by, probably thinking I went up another floor.

"Excuse me. Do you have an appointment?"

Turning, I find a girl close in age to me, glaring. There are other people in the room who look just as annoyed, too. My bad.

"Sorry. Wrong room." I leave, closing the door behind me.

I'm on high alert as I take the elevator to the first floor. Thankfully, there are other students, so I'm not alone. I manage to stay in the middle of the group as we exit the lift. The man in all-black is nowhere to be found, so I rush past the group of students and make my way outside. My brief detour got rid of the guy, but it's also put me behind schedule, so I hurry across the campus.

The closer I get to my building, the more the feeling returns. What if the man is out there, watching me? What do I do then? My building comes into sight, and I actually whimper as I climb the stairs. The hairs on the back of my neck are raised and my instincts scream for me to run. I risk a glance over my shoulder, but don't see a damn thing. There are emergency phones every hundred feet on the campus, but will that be enough to save me if someone tries to get me? What if he has a gun? What if—

"Stop being stupid."

A deep male voice asks, "Sorry?"

Turning forward, I stare at the most handsome man I've ever seen in my life. He's tall, like at least a foot taller than me, has long, dark hair that's pulled back, and is built like an ox. Good freaking lord, this man is enormous. His eyes are the color of whisky, and his lips are full, begging to be kissed. I shake my head, trying to knock myself from the stupor this man put me in.

"Crap. Sorry. I wasn't talking to you."

He looks around. "We're the only two people here."

My cheeks burn. "I was talking to myself."

"Do that a lot?"

I laugh, realizing how silly I must have sounded to him. "More than I should."

He holds out his hand. "I'm Henri."

"Nice to meet you."

"Not going to tell me your name?"

"No."

"No? Damn. Okay. Well, mystery lady, it was nice meeting you."

He steps around me, reaching for the same door that I was about to go through.

"Are you a student?"

He laughs, and I feel it deep in my belly. "Ah, no."

With that, he keeps walking, disappearing where the hallway splits. And what do I do? I stand there smiling like an idiot. The feeling of being watched is gone, which definitely helps my mood. Seriously, I need to get it together. No one is watching me. And all I'm doing is making myself look like a fool with my overactive imagination. Case in point —Henri.

I'm still smiling as I make my way to the lecture hall. Kyle is already inside and waves me over. We've known each other since high school but didn't hang out until finding ourselves in the same class this year. Kyle is... Kyle. He's a bit taller than me with sandy blond hair that he keeps cut close to his scalp. He says it's because his dad started balding around our age, and he wants to be ready. His eyes are dark, and his lips are full. He used to play football in high school, but has definitely fallen victim to the freshmen fifteen, even though he's technically a sophomore. He's one of those guys that hasn't adjusted very well from being the king of the crop to a small fish in a big pond. His words, not mine.

I sit next to him, pulling out my books. My notes are still damp, but I'll have to make do until I can buy a new notebook.

"Wasn't sure if you were going to make it."

"Mrs. McCarthy was running late. I almost had to bring Belle."

He crinkles his nose. "I'm glad you didn't."

I try not to hold it against him that he doesn't like kids. I mean, I'm not sure if I like kids, either, but I love my siblings. Someone calls out his name, asking if he's going to a party at the end of the week.

"Hell yeah I am." To me, he says, "I was going to tell you about it, but figured you wouldn't be able to go. It's at one of the frat houses."

I'm off this upcoming weekend, so, in theory, I could go. But hanging around a bunch of drunk college kids doesn't sound very appealing.

"Yeah, I won't be going."

He sighs. "I miss you, Dove. Sometimes I feel like you don't want to be my girlfriend."

His comment makes me feel like shit, as it usually does. One thing I've learned about Kyle is that he is a master manipulator. He knows what to say to people to get what he wants. And I have a pretty good idea what he wants.

"If you come to the party, we can find a room to crash in. Have some alone time."

There it is— his true motive. He's been trying to get in my pants since we started dating, but I've been firm. I don't want a million notches on my bedpost. I want meaningful ones. Something he can't seem to get through his head.

Before I can answer, the doors slam shut, and the room goes silent. Professor Westbrook is never on time, and he certainly doesn't close the doors, so this has everyone's attention. Someone in the front row turns and mouths, *oh my god,* to her friend sitting behind me. What on earth is going on?

And then I get my answer.

Henri walks up to the podium, looking like he owns the room. I swear every female and some males in the room are drooling. He's rolled up the sleeves to his dress shirt, putting his muscular forearms on display. I can't say that I've ever noticed that body part before. I have now.

He speaks into the microphone, and goosebumps lift on my skin. Why didn't I notice how deep and gravelly his voice was outside?

"Good afternoon. I'm Professor Gastov. Professor Westbrook couldn't make it today, so I will be taking over his class."

I've never seen so many people interested in what was being said. This is a blow-off class for most people. Heck, a lot of the students only show up for test days. But everyone hangs on to each word that Henri says. *Henri.* My cheeks feel warm. Why didn't he introduce himself as a professor? Our gazes meet and heat spreads across my cheeks. His eyes twinkle as he directs everyone to open their textbooks. Is he laughing at me? I glance at Kyle to see if he notices. Thankfully, he doesn't.

The hour flies by, much to my dismay.

Henri calls out, "I'll be available in Professor Westbrook's office for a bit if anyone has questions. See you all tomorrow."

Tomorrow? Does that mean he'll be covering for Professor Westbrook then, too? I feel almost giddy with excitement until Kyle ruins everything by speaking.

"I don't like that guy. What kind of professor dresses like

that? I ought to file a complaint with the head of the department."

"Why would you do that? I enjoyed the class."

"You and every other female."

"Are you jealous?"

"Don't be ridiculous." He stands. "Come on. I want a coffee before my next class."

This is our normal routine. After class, we get a drink, and then he goes into his next class while I study. I'm still kind of annoyed at him, and there was a part of the lesson that made little sense.

"You go ahead. There were some things I didn't understand."

"Are you fucking serious right now?"

He asks loud enough that a few people glance our way.

"Yes, I'm serious. Come with me if you don't believe me."

He sighs. "Whatever. I'm going. Call me when you're done. Or don't. I don't care."

He stomps off like a spoiled brat, and I gather my things. I wasn't lying when I said I had some questions. Math isn't my strong suit, and I've found that if I don't understand something, then I fall behind quickly. And I really don't want to retake this class next semester. In the hallway, I make my way toward Professor Westbrook's office. Unsurprisingly, there's a long line of people waiting to see Henri. A few of the girls even put on lipstick before entering his office. The line moves slowly, and I use the time to highlight the parts of my notes that I'm unsure about. By the time I reach the door, it's been over an hour.

Henri calls out, "Office hours are over."

The three girls in front of me groan but get out of line. I'm torn. If I wait until tomorrow, there's a chance that I won't understand the topic. Inhaling, I tap on the door.

"Professor Gastov? I'm sorry to bother, but I really need some help with this."

He looks up from his computer and gives me a slow smile that does things to me. "Is that so? By all means, mystery lady, please come in."

I'm flustered as I step into the office. Right away, I get a hint of his cologne. It literally makes my mouth water. Clamping my lips together, I slide into the seat across from his desk and put my notebook on top.

"I marked the parts that didn't make sense." My cheeks feel warm. "I know it's probably something very simple, but I'm terrible at math."

Leaning forward, he pulls my notebook across the desk and looks over it.

"You're decimal needs to be moved here." He points. "And that will solve this one."

He then launches into an explanation for each item that I have highlighted. Not only that, but he jots down a few practice questions for me to work on. Not once does he make me feel stupid. By the time we work our way through my list, another hour has passed.

"I'm so sorry for holding you up," I say as I gather my notebook and shove it into my bag. "I'm sure you have another class to get ready for."

He smiles. "No need to apologize."

God, is it hot in here or is it just me?

"Dove," I blurt out.

"Pardon?"

"You asked my name earlier. It's Dove. Dove Potts."

"Nice to meet you, Dove."

I laugh nervously. "Nice to meet you, too, Professor."

"Henri." He eyes me. "Call me Henri, Dove."

I'm like one smile away from melting onto the floor, so I back up toward the door.

"It was a great class. See you tomorrow. Oh! And thanks for all the help." And then I all but run out of the office.

I don't stop until I reach the bus stop that will take me to the train station. What in the heck was that? I don't react like that to guys, much less to my professors. My body is still warm, and my nipples press against my bra. Thank god I had a jacket on. Otherwise, Henri would have been able to tell how aroused I was. My eyes shut. I need to get it together. I have a boyfriend for crying out loud. Crap! I pull out my phone and cringe at the amount of text messages there are. There's twenty, and each one gets angrier and angrier. The last one pisses me off.

**Kyle: When you're done slobbing his knob, call me. I want my jacket back.**

I call him, waiting for him to answer. When he doesn't, I leave him a voicemail.

"First, how dare you imply that I would give our professor a blow job. Second, I invited you to come with me to his office. Third, you're being an asshole. Don't call me until you're ready to apologize."

I end the call only to find a woman near me clapping.

"You tell him, girl!"

I give her a weak smile and drop my phone into my bag. Seriously, what is Kyle's deal? I'm still stewing over his comments when I pick up the kids and take them home. Chip rambles on about what he learned at school while I make dinner.

Everything is going great until my father storms in, knocking over a chair. I can tell by the look in his eye that he's in a mean mood.

"Chip, take your homework to our room, please."

Chip glances between my father and me, but does as I've asked. I'm so thankful Belle is in her crib. One less thing to worry about. Even from here, I can smell the alcohol on my father.

"Dinner is almost ready."

"I don't give a shit about dinner."

He moves, so he has me blocked between his body and the stove. Heat from the flames lick at my back, but I don't dare move an inch.

"I'm so sick and tired of working my ass off all day and coming home to this fucking mess." His rancid breath makes my stomach turn. "If you can't do your job, then maybe you should get your shit and leave."

"Dad, you've had a long day. I can bring you a plate if you want to sit in your chair."

He backhands me so hard that my head whips to the side.

"I don't need a little cunt to tell me what to do. In fact, I could teach you a thing or two."

I flinch, and that's where everything goes wrong. I should know better by now. He thrives on knowing he scares me. That he can hurt me. I try to dart from the kitchen, but he knocks me to the floor as his fists hit me from every angle. I pray that Chip doesn't come out. My father hasn't hit him yet, but each day I know we get closer to that line being crossed.

"You stupid cunt. You're no good to me. I ought to get rid of you. Sell you to the highest bidder."

A kick lands on my side, and I cry out.

"I bet you'd go for at least a grand. Maybe that's what I'll do. Sell you so I don't have to see your face ever again."

He always says unhinged things when he gets like this, but this is the first time he's said he wants to sell me. Every fiber in my body screams that this is different. He's thought about it. Why else would he say it? Before I can dwell on it too much, he kicks me in the side of the head, and everything goes dark.

Too bad I just don't know how to die.

# 3

*Dove*

I wake up alone and on the floor. The food on the stove is burned, and I hear Belle crying. Shoving myself off the floor, I bite back a whimper of pain as I turn off the gas on the stove. There's a dark voice deep inside of my head that taunts me, telling me I should turn it back on, but make sure the flame is off. Once the apartment fills with gas, we'll all just go to sleep, and this will be over. But I can't do that.

I *won't*.

Everything hurts, and I don't want to scare Chip when I go back to our room. I don't need a mirror to know I look like shit. Shoving my pain aside, I make two peanut butter and jelly sandwiches and pour a glass of milk for Chip. Quietly, I make Belle a bottle and bring the powdered formula with me. It wouldn't be the first time I've used the water in the bathroom to make a bottle just to avoid my father.

Gathering everything on a tray, I make my way to my room, slipping silently into the room. Belle is in her crib, crying. Chip is nowhere to be found. For a moment, I panic. Did my father get him? Is he hurt?

"Chip?" I whisper. "Are you in here?"

There's movement under the bed and he crawls out. His eyes are red, as if he's been crying. God, I hope he didn't see our father hitting me.

"I brought you a PB and J sandwich. I thought we could have a picnic in here."

"I'm not hungry. Can I go to bed?"

"Sure, buddy. Want me to tuck you in?"

He shakes his head and climbs into the bed, pulling the blanket over his head. I feel like shit, but I can understand not wanting to talk right now. Belle cries a bit louder, so I put the tray on the nightstand and carry her bottle with me. Lifting her hurts, but I try not to let her feel the tension in my body. I read somewhere that babies can pick up on your mood, and I never want to do anything to make her, or Chip, feel bad.

She latches onto the bottle, holding it with her hands. I can't believe how big she's getting. I sit in the chair next to the window, looking out while she feeds. My thoughts are all over the place because I know that it's dangerous to focus on a single thought right now. So, I zone out while she fills her belly. After a quick diaper change, I put her in her crib and then slip into bed, careful not to wake Chip.

I'm not sure how long I lie there, on alert to every little sound throughout the apartment. Each hour that passes without my father coming into the room is a blessing. Eleven. Midnight. One. Two. Three. Four. Finally, the need to sleep overrules everything, and my eyes shut.

Belle wakes me up right on schedule at six. She's letting out small whimpers that means she's ready to eat again. I don't know if my father is still around, but I sure as hell don't want to give him fuel to come in here and hurt me some more. Or, god forbid, hurt one of the kids.

Chip is still sleeping as I gingerly pull myself out of bed and cross the room. Belle coos when she sees me. I'm lucky that she's a sweet-tempered baby, mostly.

"Hi honey," I whisper. "Are you ready for your ba-ba?"

She kicks her legs like she understands me. Lifting her proves to be a problem, but I work through the pain that shoots from my wrist, up my arm, and radiates into my shoulder. Holding Belle close, I close my eyes as I rock her. Mrs. McCarthy said she knew of a room that would be available to rent soon. It's smaller than the room I'm in now and costs more, but it will be safe. I told her no at first, but now I think I should consider it. I have to get the kids out of here before he takes out his anger on them.

Quietly, I open the door an inch. His door is still closed, which means he's likely passed out. Carrying Belle to the bathroom, I close and lock the door. Belle is happy to sit in her bath chair while I get ready for the day.

I don't know the woman looking back at me.

Each time I see her, I hate her a bit more.

My eyes water as I take in the damage. My cheek is bruised, a reddish and purple map of my father's damage. It spans from my temple to my mouth. My lip is scabbed from where he busted it. God, it's so tender. I already know my arm is hurt, so I'm not surprised to see bruises marring my skin. My wrist is swollen. If I had insurance, I'd go have it looked at. No, that's not true. I don't want to draw attention to myself and raise questions that I shouldn't answer.

All I want to do is take a shower, but I know I don't have time. Not if I'm actually going to make it to class today. As tempting as it is to skip, I know I can't. For one, my father is still here. Two, I can't afford to get behind. Sighing, I open the cabinet and pull out my make-up bag. I know I cannot cover all the bruising, but maybe I can make it look a bit better.

By the time I'm finished, I'm almost in tears. The foundation shade is too light to cover much. Even with my hair down, I still look like I've been beaten up. But there's no chance in hell that I'm going to hang around here, so I pick up Belle and make my way back to my room. I change, putting on a long-sleeve shirt and jeans. Too bad I don't own a turtleneck shirt. It would hide the bruising going up my neck. My hoodie will have to do for now.

Chip wakes up as I'm changing Belle. His eyes are wide as he stares at me.

"Are you okay?"

I nod, turning my head so he can't see the tears threatening to spill. "I'll be fine."

"Did Dad do that?"

I don't know what to say. He's six. He doesn't deserve to know what a piece of shit our father is, but he's also smart. I nod again.

His voice is small as he asks, "Is it because I left my toys on the table?"

This time I turn to him. "No, buddy. This isn't your fault, and it's not mine either. Dad has a drinking problem, and sometimes when he gets mad, he takes it out on other people."

"Will he take it out on me?" His lower lip quivers.

"I'd never let him hurt you."

He throws his arms around my waist. "I don't want him to hurt you, either. Or Belle."

I hug him back. "You're a brave boy. Belle and I are lucky to have you."

"I'm not brave. When I heard Dad yelling last night, I hid."

"Were you in here with Belle?"

He nods.

"Then you were being brave because you kept her safe. And I'm so glad you were in here, with her."

He sniffles. "Really?"

"Really. Now, let's get dressed. I think I want donuts for breakfast."

I shouldn't spend any extra money right now, but we need to get out of the apartment, and school drop-off doesn't start for an hour.

"Can I get one with sprinkles?"

"Of course."

He smiles and changes his clothes while I make sure his backpack, Belle's diaper bag, and my school bag are packed. When everyone is dressed, we make our way out of the apartment, being as quiet as we can.

Mrs. McCarthy can't hide the horrified expression on her face when she sees me.

She takes Belle's carrier and asks, "Are you okay?"

"I'll be fine." The lie rolls right off my tongue. "Sorry we're so early."

Her gaze searches mine. "Don't be sorry. Look, I know it's not much, but I have a couch that you are more than welcome to sleep on."

My eyes water, and I nod. "I might take you up on that."

"Good." One of her kids calls her name, and she glances over her shoulder before saying, "Well, I better get back in there before there's cereal on the ceiling."

I laugh, knowing she's mostly kidding. Her kids are great, just like her. I take Chip's hand in mine, and we make our way outside.

"Brr. Do you think it's going to snow?" Chip asks as he skips along next to me.

"I hope not. It's too early for snow."

He launches into a story that I half-heartedly listen to as we make our way to a nearby *Dunkin' Donuts* store. Chip gets his sprinkle donut and a chocolate milk while I grab an iced coffee.

"Do we have time to sit?"

"We do."

He picks out a table by the window, so we can people watch. Chip loves watching people, making observations about them. And I'll do anything to make my little brother happy.

"Oh, look! That lady has a dog in her purse. Can we get a dog?"

"We don't have a yard for it to play in."

He frowns. "Yeah, you're right. Beckham has a fish. Can I get a fish?"

"Maybe."

"I know what that means."

I smile. "What does it mean?"

"Maybe means *no*." He pauses. "Is it because we're poor?"

"Who said we're poor?"

"One kid on the team. He said that's why my mom left. Is that why she went to heaven? Because she was tired of not having nice things?"

Kids can be such little assholes!

"Your mom was sick, and that's why she went to heaven. As for being poor, do you think we're poor?"

He shrugs. "Sometimes. We don't have cool things, like Beckham."

He's not wrong there. One day he will know just how

poor we are, but today is not that day.

"We have a warm place to stay, food to eat, and clothes to wear. Some people don't even have that."

"I know, I know." He gives me an ornery smile. "It would still be cool if I was a prince or something."

"A prince, huh?"

"Yeah. Then we'd live in a castle, have lots of toys, and no one would be mean to me because I'd have a bodyguard."

I wonder if I should be alarmed that he thinks he needs a bodyguard.

But then he says, "And I'd have enough money to hire the Avengers to come to school with me, too."

"You've given this a lot of thought."

He wipes his mouth with the sleeve of his shirt. "Yup."

"So, if you're a prince, does that make Belle and I princesses?"

"I think so. Or you might be a queen."

"A queen, huh?"

"Yeah."

"Does that mean I marry a king?"

He nods. "And guess what?"

"What?"

"He makes sure that Dad can't hurt you anymore."

My eyes mist over. "Then I hope you are a prince. But, today, you're still Chip Potts, and you have to go to school."

He groans playfully but throws away his trash. Hand in hand, we make our way outside. It's amazing how talking to my little brother can make me feel so much better. As we get closer to the school, I pull up the hood on the hoodie, hoping to hide some of the bruising. Thankfully, Chip sees Beckham and tells me goodbye as he runs over to his friend. I manage to slip away without getting looks from anyone.

Since I have time to kill, I decide to walk. What I'm

really doing is trying to figure out what I'm going to tell people when they ask what happened. Like Kyle. I'm sure he'll have plenty to say. Digging into my pocket, I pull out my phone. He never texted me after class the other day because he doesn't think he did anything wrong. But I should give him a heads-up.

**Me:** Hey.

**Kyle:** Hey.

**Me:** Are you at your place?

**Kyle:** No, I swung by my parent's house to do some laundry.

**Me:** Are you skipping class today?

**Kyle:** What are you, my mother?

**Me:** You don't have to be a dick. It was just a question.

**Kyle:** Sure.

**Kyle:** To answer your 'question', yes, I'm skipping class.

**Kyle:** After my girlfriend was a bitch to me, I went out with some friends and had too much to drink.

**Kyle:** The last thing I want to do is sit in a classroom with her and the guy she probably fucked.

My face flames in anger, but he's not done.

**Kyle:** So, yes, I'm skipping class. And after my laundry is done, I'm going out with some friends again.

**Kyle:** You know... people who KNOW how to have fun.

**Kyle:** And just so we're clear, everyone thinks you want to fuck the professor. Good job with letting everyone know what a little slut you are.

I grit my teeth, which only causes pain in my face. What an asshole!

**Me:** You know what? You can go fuck yourself.

**Me:** We're done.

**Kyle:** Good.

**Kyle: And guess what?**

**Kyle: I've been fucking other people all along, so no loss to me.**

**Kyle: Lose my number, sweetie.**

I'm close to raging right here in the middle of the street. I can handle being called a lot of things, but sweetie? Hell no. Maybe it's because Chip's mom used to call me that, and not sweetly. When someone calls me that, I know what they mean. It's the southern equivalent of *bless your heart*. There's nothing *nice* about it.

I block Kyle's number in my contacts and then block him on social media. I don't have time to deal with him or his shit. I mean, he's basically doing me a favor. It's not like our relationship was going anywhere. I'm still irritated as I get on a bus headed toward the campus. Thankfully, no one looks my way. Sometimes, being able to blend in is a blessing.

Once I'm off the bus, I make my way across the campus. I'm deep in thought when I enter the building and head to the lecture hall. Should I take the kids and stay with Mrs. McCarthy tonight? Will my father even think of looking there for us? She has kids of her own, and I don't want to put her or them in danger. Okay, so I can't go there. I wonder if I can find a cheap motel room for a few nights. Pulling out my phone, I log into my bank account.

Well, that's out of the question, too. I don't have enough money for that, and I don't want to dig into my emergency stash of money unless I have to. Crap. Maybe it's time to swallow my pride and look into a shelter. The thing that worries me is that I don't have legal guardianship over Chip and Belle. If I take them to a shelter, will someone try to take them from me? My dad hasn't hurt them yet, so it will be my word against his.

Each potential solution only brings more heartache for me. I either can't afford it or there's a chance that I'll lose my siblings. There's a part of me that wonders if they wouldn't be better off without me. They might get placed somewhere together with a family who will love them and be able to take care of them. But the news is riddled with stories of kids who are abused in the system. I'd never forgive myself if something happened to them.

Looking at my phone, I type in the club's name by my house. Neverland. Maybe they're hiring. If they pay enough, it might be something worth looking into. It's a brothel, but surely there are jobs there that don't require sleeping with someone. Right?

Suddenly, a door opens right in front of me, and I walk into it before I can stop myself. I fall right on my butt, groaning.

"Dove? Are you okay?"

Groaning, I look up, finding Henri looking down at me with horror etched on his face. The expression worsens when he gets a good look at me.

"What happened to you?"

I'm still a bit dazed. "How did I get on the ground?"

His eyebrows lift. "The bigger question is, what in the fuck happened to your face?"

My cheeks feel like they're on fire as I try to sit. He exhales, holding out his hand. My pride is already bruised as much as my face, so I shake my head and force myself to my feet.

"Dove, I'm only going to ask this once more. What happened?"

"Well, I believe you opened a door that I walked into while I was looking at my phone." My lips lift in a half smile as I try to take the seriousness out of the situation.

He grabs my upper arm, pulling me into his office, where he closes the door. Being this close, my senses are assaulted by all things Henri. His scent. The closeness of his body. The smell of coffee lingering in the air.

"Dove?"

Shit. Maybe I have a concussion?

"It's nothing."

"Someone used you as a punching bag." His gaze narrows. "Was it that fucker you were sitting with yesterday?"

I'm a bit shocked to hear him talking like that. Most professors try to remain... professional. At least, that's the impression I've always gotten.

"Dove."

His tone is obvious—he's getting impatient with me, and I shouldn't anger him. The funny thing is, I'm not scared. Now if my father were here...

"It wasn't Kyle."

"If it wasn't *Kyle*, then who was it?" He says Kyle's name as if it tastes bitter. Maybe it does.

"It doesn't matter. I... I shouldn't have come today."

"Wait right here. And don't even think about leaving."

He leaves the room, closing the door behind him. I stare at my hands, wondering what in the hell is happening. Should I leave while he's gone? He's going to want answers. That much is clear. That's it. I should get my things and get the heck out of here. I'm reaching for my bag when the door opens, and Henri enters, closing the door behind him. My heart pounds as we stare at each other. The urge to run is back, but my gut tells me he would chase. So, I stay as still as I can, almost holding my breath. Praying I'm not making a mistake.

# 4

*Dove*

Henri sits on the edge of his desk, facing me. God. Why does he look so yummy like this? His slacks are pulled taunt across his massive thighs. It's no wonder they don't rip right down the middle. His arms are crossed, pulling the dark grey shirt against his muscular chest. Right now, he's working his bottom lip between his fingers as he stares at me.

I want to make a smart-ass comment to take the edge off the mood in the room, but I notice the clock.

"Henri, class was supposed to start ten minutes ago."

"Class is canceled today."

"Since when?"

He lets out a small laugh. "Since we ran into each other, and I saw your face. Now, tell me who did this."

I shake my head. "It doesn't matter."

"I beg to fucking differ."

"If I tell you, then you'll want to do something about it, right?"

"Damn fucking straight."

"That's why I won't tell you." I stand. "I'm sorry for bumping into you. For what it's worth, I was looking forward to today's lesson."

"Dove, don't leave." He exhales. "Or, if you're insistent, then come with me."

"Where?"

"My apartment is nearby. We can go there and talk. Hell, I don't care if we even watch a movie."

There's so much that I need to do today, like looking for a place to stay. But I'm so tempted. I can't remember the last time I did something for just myself.

"I have to leave by four so I can pick up my siblings."

"Deal. Let's go."

Thankfully, the halls are empty as we make our way outside. He puts his hand on my lower back as we walk, and I hate that I like it. Maybe Kyle was right. Maybe I'm hoping something does happen with Henri, like a little slut.

"I don't like that frown on your face. It makes me think you're planning on running."

I snort, glancing up at him. "I will not run. Just thinking about something my ex said."

"Do I even want to know?"

I shrug. "He's mad because he thinks I blew him off the other day when I went to your office. Said some nasty things, insinuating that I was acting like a slut to get your attention."

His jaw tics. "You swear to me he isn't the one who did this?"

"He's not. I promise."

We reach a black SUV that looks expensive. He opens the passenger door, motioning for me to climb in. I do, and then I'm shocked as hell as he grabs the seat buckle, buckling me in. He even gives the strap a little tug, making sure it's nice and secure.

My face feels like it's on fire. "You didn't have to do that."

"I wanted to."

He gives me a smile that makes my lower belly feel like it's on fire and then closes the door. A moment later, he rounds the car and climbs in next to me. The interior of the SUV is spacious, but it doesn't feel like it at the moment. Not at all. He puts his arm on the center console, leaning toward me as the SUV starts. I have an insane urge to reach over and take his hand in mine. I don't.

Soft music plays through the speakers. It's nice. But then the next song starts, and I laugh.

"Five Finger Death Punch?"

He taps his hand on the steering wheel in perfect tune with the song. "Well, since you know who they are, I'm assuming you either love them or hate them."

"Love them. They're my go-to band."

He smiles, glancing at me. "Mine, too."

We turn down a road where high-rises line each side of the street. I'm surprised when we go into a parking garage under the building.

"You live here?"

This building is owned by the Di Bello Family. Even if everyone in the city didn't know it just because it's common knowledge, the Family crest on the side is a huge giveaway. The rose dripping blood. Romantic and yet a warning, too.

Henri says, "Got a good deal on it."

"I'm surprised. I didn't think the Di Bello's were known for being generous."

He snorts. "They're not, but they owed me."

"Oh?"

"Nope, sweetheart. That's not how this works. I'm not telling you shit until you tell me who hurt you."

That makes my lips clamp shut. Guess we're not going to talk then.

He parks the car in a reserved spot near the elevators.

"Sit still. I'll open your door."

"You don't have to."

"I *want* to."

I nod because I'm too shocked to do anything else. No one has ever offered to open a door for me. Much less act insulted that I might have to do it on my own. He climbs out of the SUV and jogs around the back of the vehicle, opening my door. I smile as he holds out his hand. I take it, noticing the jolt of electricity that passes between us. I really need to pull it together. He's way out of my league. Heck, he's just doing this to be nice.

He gives me a small smile and leads the way. There are two lifts, and he goes to the one that requires his thumbprint for the door to open.

"No eye scan?" I tease.

"Only on my front door."

The elevator rises high into the sky. My ears pop as they adjust, and I feel a bit dizzy. When the doors open, we step out. There's only one door.

"You own the entire floor?"

"I do."

He goes to the door. Oh, my goodness. I guess he wasn't kidding. There's a small pad next to the door that scans his eyes and beeps. The door swings open.

"After you."

Am I crazy for going home with someone I don't know? Sure, he's a professor at my college, but I don't know him. I glance up and meet his gaze. I might not know him, but I know he's not a bad person. He doesn't have the same malicious look in his eyes that my father does, and he doesn't look at me like he wants to hurt me. So, I walk into the house.

It's an open-floor concept with a floor to ceiling window with a view of Lake Michigan. The walls are dark, and there are beams on the high ceilings, reminding me of a pub. His furniture is brown leather and I almost expect to find a fur rug in front of the stone-covered fireplace. The decorations on the walls are interesting. Old muskets hang in rows. They must be important. Why else would he display them?

He says, "These were my grandfather's. Had to fight a cousin for them, but the old man wanted me to have them."

"Did he like to hunt?"

He looks pained for a moment before snorting. "If it ran, he liked to hunt."

He motions for me to join him on the couch. I sit next to him, and I think he's pleased as his arm goes around my shoulder, pulling me close.

"His house was massive. My cousins and I used to spend the summers there. We'd run the grounds until we were worn out. My favorite place was this hidden meadow with a creek that ran through it." He smiles. "I could spend hours out there. My older cousin liked to spend time in the library. That room used to creep me out, but I never said anything."

"Why?"

"Why did it creep me out, or why didn't I say anything?"

"Both."

He looks at the guns. "The library was dark and foreboding. It smelled like musty books and old people."

I laugh. "Old people?"

"I guess like baby powder and something else." He

shakes his head. "I could get past all of that, but it was the mounted heads on the wall that really got to me."

"Heads from the game he killed?"

He nods. "They hung there, trophies to his cruelness. He loved exotic game best, so there were plenty of elephants, lions, and any other beast you can imagine. There were also a few stuffed animals. I think those were the worst. Frozen in time for eternity in min-run."

I say, "I can see how that could creep a kid out. Why didn't you say anything?"

"My grandfather was an asshole. He didn't mellow out until we got older and could knock him on his ass if needed. Had he known that I was scared, he would have used it against me. Hell, my older cousin would have, too."

I touch his arm. "I'm sorry."

"Don't be. I got out of that house and from under the thumb of the family. They were so fucking mad when I became a teacher. Said I could be anything, and that I was wasting my life by being an educator. Never mind that it takes a master's degree to become a professor and never mind that I paid for it on my own."

"Well, I think it's great that you branched out on your own."

"What about you, Dove? What scares you?"

I close my eyes. "I'm afraid to tell you."

"Why? Do I scare you?"

"A bit," I admit. "But not in a bad way."

"Good."

I turn so I can see him. "If I tell you who hurt me, you have to swear that you won't do anything."

"I'm not sure I can make that kind of promise, but I swear I'll do my best."

I know it's probably not enough. I should get up and

leave, but I don't want to. He scares me, but he also makes me feel safe. It's confusing, but I decide to trust my gut.

"My dad has always had... issues. He drinks too much and spends all of his money on his addictions."

"He hurt you?"

I nod once.

"I know it's not safe there, and I know that one day he'll get angry at my little brother and maybe even my little sister." I blink back the tears in my eyes. "That's why I'm going to school, even though it's going to take forever for me to get a degree. And that's why I work three jobs. Because one of these days I'm going to have enough money to get my siblings and myself out of his house and never look back."

He pulls me close, kissing the top of my head. "I'll make sure of it."

I want to ask what he means, but I don't because I feel so freaking secure. At the moment, I don't care about anything except that he's still holding me close and that I feel safe. Right now, I'm not Dove, the protector of all. I'm just a woman being held by a man. A very handsome man whose arms feel like heaven.

"Do you want to watch a movie? We can order in lunch and just chill."

I grin. "Are you asking me to Netflix and chill, Professor?"

He grins back. "Yes."

Holy hotness.

"Yeah, let's find something to watch."

He leans away for a moment, grabbing the remote from the side table. I'm pleased when he puts his arm back around me. He lets me pick what we watch and laughs when I choose a murder documentary.

"Interesting pick. Should I be worried?"

"They help me unwind."

"Is that what you're doing?"

"Yeah."

He gives me a lazy smile. "When I unwind, I usually take off my work clothes and put on gym shorts."

My cheeks burn. "I don't have any gym shorts with me."

"You can borrow a t-shirt. It will probably fit you like a dress, but I'm sure it will be comfortable."

My brain screams that this is dangerous territory, but I can't stop myself from asking, "And you'll put on your gym shorts?"

"Sure will."

"Okay."

He stands, pulling me to my feet. We're silent as he leads me past the massive kitchen, down a hallway, and into his room. I know it's his because his scent assaults my nose right away. Somehow, I manage to resist inhaling. The temptation is there. Big time.

The décor in here is like the living room. Dark. Masculine. Sexy. We pass his massive bed and enter a spacious walk-in closet. One side has suits and dress wear. The other side is empty, as if he's waiting for someone to fill it. Or maybe he had someone, and she's gone. He pads to the built-in dresser at the back of the closet and opens a drawer, pulling out light grey shorts. A small groan escapes my mouth. Of course, they're grey. From the next drawer, he pulls out a white t-shirt, and tosses it to me.

"Bathroom is through the other door. I'll change in my room to give you some privacy."

I nod, brushing past him to go to the bathroom. It's freaking beautiful. White tiles with golden grout line the floor and walls. The accessories are golden, too. There's a double vanity with his and hers sinks. My favorite thing is the massive walk-in shower that looks like it could hold ten people. I'm assuming the toilet is behind the other closed door. Rich people. The thought has me smiling. I once saw a TikTok that said if you could touch the sink, shower, and door all while sitting on the toilet, then you were poor. I laughed at the time because it was so accurate. No touching anything here unless it's your intended goal.

There's a tap on the door. "You doing okay in there, Dove?"

"Just debating jumping in the shower and trying out the rain showerhead."

He laughs. "If you do, let me know. The water knobs can be a bit tricky."

An image of him seeing me naked crosses my mind, and my body heats in response.

"I'm just kidding. I'll be out in a moment."

Before I can talk myself out of it, I take off my hoodie, shirt, and jeans. I glimpse myself in the mirror and flinch. The bruising is black and purple now, making it look twenty times worse. I look disgusting. There's no way Henri would want me. Not when I look like this. Grabbing his shirt, I pull it over my head. He wasn't lying when he said it would look like a dress on me. It's comfortable and doesn't hurt my skin the way my clothes did. Pulling my hair into a ponytail, I exit the bathroom.

Henri is leaning against his bedpost, phone in hand. He looks angry, but the look fades when he sees me, but I barely notice because he looks so good. He's wearing the grey shorts and nothing else. His muscular chest is on display, and I'm surprised at the dark dusting of hair. Normally, I'd say that I like a guy with a smooth chest, but he looks so handsome that I might just have to reconsider.

He looks up, pausing. "Damn."

"What?"

"It's going to be hard to keep my hands to myself."

His words make my cheeks feel warm, but I like it.

"Do you like pizza?"

"We live in Chicago. Of course I like pizza."

"Deep dish?"

I nod. "Yeah."

"Thank god. That was going to be a deal breaker for me."

I laugh, following him to the living room.

"What if I had said I liked New York style?"

He makes a pained sound. "Then you would have gone from a solid ten to a six."

"A six! Dang, you're a hard man to please Henri.

He grins. "You have no idea."

Why, oh why, is that so freaking sexy?

"Let's order the food. I grabbed some blankets while you were changing so we can veg out."

Sure enough, there are some fuzzy blankets on the couch. He sits in his spot, patting the seat next to him. When I sit, he covers both of us with a blanket. Since I'm wearing his shirt now, I can feel the heat coming off his body in waves. I snuggle closer to him.

"You good with pepperoni?"

"Yeah. Can we get some root beer to go with it?"

His eyebrow lifts. "Root beer?"

"My little brother likes it. It kind of grew on me."

"Root beer it is. Anything else? Dessert?"

I feel warm. "I'm good with anything you want."

"Anything?"

I nod, and he exhales through his nose, reminding me of a bull. But then he turns his attention to his phone as he orders the food. Maybe I misread the situation? I'm still doubting myself as he drops his phone on the table next to him and starts the documentary. We're silent as the narrator sets the scene of a woman who killed her lover. Maybe I should leave. I mean, something is different. Was it my answer about dessert? I'm about ready to hop right off the couch when his hand goes to my knee.

"Relax, Dove. I can turn the lights off if that will help?"

Do I want to sit here in the dark with him? Yeah, I kind of do.

"Okay."

He doesn't look at me as he lifts another control with his free hand. A moment later, shades lower, leaving the room in near darkness. The thing I notice the most, though, is that his hand is still on my leg.

"How old are you, Dove?"

His question takes me by surprise. "Twenty-two. Why?"

"Just want to make sure I'm not about to break some laws by having you here like this."

My pulse pounds in my neck, but I can also feel it throbbing between my legs. "Like what?"

"I can feel the heat coming off your sweet pussy right now and it's making it hard to think."

My lips part and he smirks.

"Tell me I'm wrong. Tell me that if I were to reach into your panties that I wouldn't find them soaking wet."

I was wet before, but his words send another rush of moisture between my legs.

I say, "I can't."

"Fuck. Tell me this is madness, Dove. I swear to god I'll move to another seat, and we can forget this is happening."

"I can't do that, either."

He groans, sounding tormented. I never do things like this. I'm always the responsible one. The one who does what they're supposed to and would never consider fooling around with their professor. Screw that. I want to live. Reaching under the blanket, I take his hand and guide it toward my panties.

"I want you to see how wet you make me."

He grips my panties. "Last chance, little girl."

And what do I do?

I lean in and whisper, "Give it to me, Daddy."

# 5

*Dove*

My cheeks flame as soon as I say the words, but they can't be taken back. Henri doesn't look disgusted, though. He looks like he wants to eat me alive. I wonder if I should tell him I don't have a lot of experience? I mean, what if he wants something that I'm not ready to do?

He pulls me onto his lap, so that I'm straddling him. Oh my goodness. If that's what I think it is, then Henri is very blessed indeed. His bulge presses against my panties. There's just enough pressure that it feels good. Without thinking, I rub myself against him. We both groan. His dark gaze holds mine as he trails a path up my thigh and between my legs. My breath hitches when he pushes the cotton material aside and runs his finger through my folds.

"Look at that. My little girl is soaked. Is that sweet cream all for me?"

He continues to stroke me, dragging his finger to my clit, where he circles it until I'm rocking against his hand and his hard-on.

"That feels so good," I breathe out.

"Yeah?"

"Yeah."

"I bet it tastes good, too."

He pulls his hand from my panties. I whimper again, and he grins as he puts his finger into his mouth.

"Fucking delicious."

"Can I... can I taste?"

His hips arch, pressing his cock against my mound. "You want a taste?"

"Yes."

"Yes, what?"

"Yes, Daddy."

He grunts, slipping his hand into my panties. I'm so wet that I can hear the juicy sound of my arousal as he moves his fingers. My lower stomach is tingling, and I know an orgasm is building. I rock against his hand and groan when he pulls his hand from my panties.

"Open up."

When my lips part, he slips two fingers inside. I can taste myself on him, and it sends another wave of moisture between my legs. I suck on his fingers until they're clean.

"See? Your cream tastes so fucking good."

He pulls his fingers from my mouth, and I pout.

"I wasn't done."

"Your hot mouth is driving me nuts. I'm about to blow my load."

To emphasize his point, he rocks into me again. Deep down, I know this is madness. We don't know each other. He's my professor. He's older. I just broke up with my boyfriend. The list goes on and on. None of it matters, though. Not here, in the room's darkness.

"Daddy, can we take our clothes off?"

"We sure can."

He taps me on the hip to stand. I do, and he has my shirt pulled over my head and tossed to the side before my feet even touch the ground. My bra is next and then my panties.

"Fuck, you're fucking perfect."

I know I'm not. I'm covered in bruises, and my body is too curvy. Heck, at my last appointment with my doctor, he said I was obese, and then told me why I needed to lose weight. I kindly reminded him I was there for an ear infection and that if he couldn't do his job that I would find someone who could, which shut him up. But I don't feel ugly or fat right now. Not when Henri dwarfs over me, making me feel small and fragile. He reaches out, palming one of my breasts. My nipple puckers as he thumbs it. A needy ache spreads throughout my body and I reach out to his waistband.

"You have on too many clothes."

He smirks at me. "Is that so?"

Together, we pull his shorts down his long legs. His cock springs up, resting on his stomach. Holy crap. He's huge. Fisting himself, he sits and pats his lap. All modesty is gone as I straddle him. This time, the tip of his cock tickles my opening.

"Your greedy pussy wants Daddy's cock, doesn't it?"

I make a sound of agreement, rocking against him.

"I'm not going to fuck you today."

"Why not?"

"Because you've been through a lot, and I don't want you to regret this."

I should be glad that he's being the voice of reason, but I'm not. I just want to feel special. My eyes water as I nod my understanding.

"Don't cry, sweet girl. I'm not going to fuck you, but that doesn't mean I'm not going to make you feel good."

"You promise?"

He brushes my hair from my face. "I promise."

I rub against him. I can't help it. He doesn't stop me, though. In fact, he lifts his hips and I gasp. Feeling bold, I lean forward and kiss him. He doesn't let me down and kisses me back until I feel dizzy. And then he moves, as if we're having sex. My breath catches in my throat when his fingers dig into my hips. Not because it hurts. Because I think he wants me as much as I want him. Unlike my dealings with Kyle, Henri doesn't make me feel like this is something that I owe him. No, he acts like this is a gift. Like *I'm* a gift...

"Sweetheart, if we keep this up, I going to cum," he rumbles against my ear. "I don't mind, but I thought you might want to know before I make a mess."

I rock against him, and he groans.

"Do it. I want to know your scent is on me."

His expression is borderline pained, but he nods. "Hold on."

Reaching between us, he adjusts his cock so that it's against my nether lips. I'm so wet that I know he can feel it as he rocks his hips. We move as if we've done this a million times. My breasts brush against his chest, and the light dusting of hair makes a delicious friction that I feel like a jolt right to my core. Our heavy breathing fills the air, as well as the occasional gasp from me when it feels especially good.

"Fuck, you're so perfect," Henri praises. "I don't know how our paths never crossed before, but now that I have you, I'm not letting you go."

His words pierce my heart in the best way possible, and I

kiss him as tears leak from my eyes. There's no way he can know how much I've needed to hear those words in my life. He doesn't want to let me go. I'm not someone that's disposable. He cups my face as we kiss, but pulls back much too soon for my liking.

"What's this?" he asks, running his thumb over my tears.

"It's nothing."

"Sweetheart, you're crying. Something's wrong."

I shake my head. "It's just... it meant a lot what you said. About how you weren't going to let me go."

My face flames, but I *need* him to know.

"I mean it, too. I feel a strong connection with you, Dove. Something I haven't felt in a long time."

I nod because I feel the same way. I've never felt like this about anyone. Not Kyle. Not any of the other boys I've dated. Henri is like the sun, and I want to bask in his warmth until it consumes me. Until *he* consumes me.

I kiss him and rock my hips, needing to be as close to him as possible. His chest rumbles as he groans.

"Fuck. I'm trying to take it slow."

"What if I don't want to take it slow?"

He pulls back, staring into my eyes. "Be careful what you ask for, little girl."

I swear to god his words send a jolt through my body that has me gushing. He reaches between our bodies and drags his finger through my arousal, circling his finger around my clit. A needy sound escapes my mouth before I can stop it. It's nothing compared to the storm brewing inside my body. We're back to dry humping, but it's not enough. Not even with him playing with my clit.

"Henri," I moan.

"Tell Daddy what you need."

"You. I need you."

He slips two fingers inside of me, and I clench around him. This feels better, but it's still not what I need. He still manages to bring me higher and higher until I'm close to shattering.

"Please fuck me, Daddy. Please. Please!"

I don't even know what I'm saying. All I know is I need a release and I'm certain his cock is the only thing that will give me what I'm seeking.

"Just the tip," he growls in my ear. "I need to feel your pussy, baby."

I nod. "Yes!"

In the back of my mind, I know I'm playing a dangerous game, but I can't bring myself to care. Not when he pulls his fingers from my pussy and lines his cock at my opening. It's so thick that it scares me, but all thoughts flee when he slips the tip in. Holy shit. I feel fuller than I did when he had his fingers inside of me.

"Oh god," I moan.

"Not God. Just your Daddy." He nuzzles my neck. "I want to go in some more. Are you okay with that?"

"Yes." My voice is full of need, but I don't care.

He pulls back and I want to cry. No! But then he rocks his hips, sliding into me more than he did before. My pussy clenches around him and we both make sounds of pleasure.

"Do that again, little girl."

I do, and he rubs my clit at the same time. Without thinking, I rock against him, pulling him a bit deeper inside of me. He stretches me in a way that I've never been stretched before, and it feels so good. Goosebumps break out across my skin when he sucks on my neck on a spot that has me rushing toward my orgasm.

"Henri," I moan as I shatter.

"You're so fucking perfect," he says as he pulls back.

I'm too caught up in my orgasm to care as he flips me, so I'm lying on the couch. He spreads my legs and then holds his cock in his hand. For a moment, I pray he's going to enter me fully, but he doesn't. Instead, he jerks himself off, grunting as he finds his own pleasure. It's the most erotic thing I've ever seen, and my own body responds. Leaning forward, he pushes the tip of his cock inside of me as he comes. I can feel his hot cum painting my pussy, and I clench around him, wanting to savor the moment. Our mouths meet in a frenzied kiss as I shatter again. I love the feeling of his weight on top of me and wish that we had fucked for real.

He kisses me and says, "Dove Potts, you're in danger."

My pulse skitters. "Danger?"

"Yes. You're in danger of having me at your mercy."

A wide smile spreads across my face. "The feeling is mutual, Professor."

"Good." He brushes my hair from my face. "I didn't hurt you, did I?"

"No. I liked everything that happened. A lot."

He smiles, and it takes my breath away. "Now that's something every man loves hearing. For the record, I liked everything, too."

I moisten my lips. "I, uh, hope there will be a next time."

"Oh, there most certainly will be." He reaches between us, rubbing my sensitive clit. "I need to be inside of you the next time I cum."

"I want that, too."

We smile at each other. This is the first time that I've ever felt at ease with a man like this and it's nice. No, nice isn't the right word. He makes me feel so many things that it's hard to put them into words. But I like it. I like it a lot. His gaze goes to my lips, and my entire body tingles as I guess his train of thought. He kisses me slowly, teasing my tongue with his. I never knew kissing could be so erotic. With Kyle, it felt like a chore. With Henri, it feels like a gift.

His cock is semihard and gets harder as we kiss. I can still feel his cum dripping out of me, and I must be greedy because I already want more. Just as I'm about to suggest moving to his bed, the alarm on my phone goes off. We both groan, though this time it's for a different reason.

"I need to go, or I'll be late picking up my brother and sister."

He grips my hips, staring down at me. "You could stay."

"Henri," I sigh. "There's more to it than that."

"I know. I'm just being a selfish asshole."

"You're not selfish at all. You're the only person who's ever shown that they care about me."

Something flickers in his gaze but is gone so fast that I must have imagined it. He brushes his lips against mine and then moves off me and stands, holding out his hand. I take it and stand. When I do, I feel his cum dripping out of me. It's naughty and makes me wish I was the type of person who could shrug off my responsibilities.

"I better clean up."

The doorbell rings, and Henri lets out a laugh. "That's probably the pizza. Go change, and I'll pay the delivery person."

Cheeks flaming, I rush to his bedroom, closing the door behind me. I use the bathroom and then change into my clothes. When I look in the mirror, I realize I look different. Happier even. My lips curl into a smile before I can stop it, but then I remember that I need to get home so I can pack a bag before my dad shows up. That little dose of reality brings me out of my post-orgasm haze. I leave the bathroom, making my way back to Henri. The scent of pizza makes my stomach growl. I wish I could stay for more than one reason.

In the living room, Henri's phone dings and he glances at the screen before dropping it on the table.

He says, "I called a car for you. That way, you can take the pizza home. I'm sure your brother will like it."

"Thank you."

I keep waiting for it to feel awkward between us, but it doesn't. Instead, I feel sad because I'm about to leave.

"You're sure I can't convince you to stay?"

I want to. God, I want to stay so much, but I can't. There's so much that he doesn't know, and I don't expect him to take on my problems.

"Sadly, I need to go."

His gaze searches mine. "Fine. But I'm adding my number to your phone, and I expect you to text if you need anything."

"I can do that."

"What are you doing this weekend?"

"This weekend? I was supposed to work at the diner, but I don't think my bruises will fade by then, so I'll likely hang around the apartment."

"I want you to stay here. Bring your siblings, too. You're all invited. We can make it fun and watch movies and veg out."

His offer is so freaking tempting.

His lips brush against my forehead. "Think about it. No pressure."

"Thank you."

My phone buzzes in my pocket and I bite back a sigh. "I should go."

"Wait." He takes my phone and types. "There. Now you have my number."

"Thanks."

We smile at each other. Suddenly, I wish I didn't have to go. I wish I could get Chip and Belle and let Henri take care of us and never look back. But this isn't a fairytale, and I know that I need to plan some more before I can make any moves.

Henri tips my chin and kisses me. It feels like a promise, and I hope and pray he doesn't let me down.

"I should go."

"The doorman will show you which car is for you."

One more kiss and then I force myself to leave. He stays in the same spot as I walk out of his apartment, closing the door behind me. In the elevator, I lean against the wall, closing my eyes. I think I'm falling for Henri Gastov.

*Henri*

Dove leaves and it takes everything in my power not to grab her and tell her she's never going back to that hellhole. My fingers tingle with the need to bring pain down on the man who hurt her. Her fucking father. Maurice's report stares back at me on my phone, and I open it. I knew I wouldn't be able to read it in front of her without showing my emotions, and I didn't want to scare her.

Now? Now I want to know all about the man I'm going to murder.

*Name: David Potts*
*Age: 42*

*Current Occupation: Janitor*
*Former Occupation:*

The list is so fucking long that I have to scroll several times to get to the next line.

*Spouse(s) and long-term partner(s): Terri Lee(d), Katie Rosio(d), Sammie Josephs(d).*

"I'm seeing a fucking trend," I mutter as I go to the couch, sitting in the same spot where I had Dove spread out before me moments ago.

The next few pages are of his encounters with the law. DUIs, domestic abuse, attempted robbery, trespassing, stalking, forged checks, falsified identity. The domestic abuse part has me seeing red because I've seen his handiwork up close and personal. That's perfectly fine, because he's going to see the same treatment, tenfold.

His financial reports are next, which makes me laugh. He's a loser who can barely keep a job. He's up to his neck in debt. Hell, he doesn't even pay the rent for his apartment. No, every check is sent from Dove's account. He likes to frequent Neverland and his next favorite establishment is Casino Di Bello. My hand closes into a fist as I see how many times he visits the casino in a month. In fact, he was there yesterday. And lost everything. Is that why he beat the shit out of Dove? Because he lost a couple grand and was pissed about it?

It figures Luca would let a lowlife like David Potts back in the casino. That's how he makes his money. Smart players know the house always wins, and that it's wise to move around. Then there are people like Potts, who hope they will win a life-changing amount and come back day after day until the house takes back everything and then some. The report says that he usually arrives around four. I frown. Dove said she needed to be home by four to get her siblings.

While she's taking care of them, her father will shit away their money. Again.

I have to get Dove out of that hellhole. How do I convince her that this is a safe place to come when I know it's not? Luca will take one look at her and see the same thing I did. And he won't stop until he's broken her. My gaze goes the wall where Grandfather's muskets hang. There was more to the story than I told Dove. Things I've spent years trying to forget. My eyes close. Things I've spent years trying to deny. Even thinking about it now is dangerous. The old feelings are there, lurking beneath the surface. The self-loathing and bitterness of who I was forced to become. But there's also a part of me that misses who I used to be. Who wants nothing more than to—

Cursing, I jump to my feet. I'm going to take a fucking shower and then I'm going to figure out what to do about Dove. I've waited years to find someone like her. Now that I have, I'm going to do everything in my power to make her mine.

# 6

## Di Bello

*Henri*

After looking into David Potts, one thing is clear. My cousin is setting him up for something, and I have an inkling what it is. My fist clenches as I get out of my car, making my way into a place I try to avoid as much as possible. Men look my way as I pass, some surprised to see me. Others, not so much. No one dares to say anything, though. I might not come here often, but I'm still high ranking. The spare to the heir, if you will.

My gaze drifts upward to the second floor. The lights are off in the office. Good. I don't want to see that prick if I can avoid it. Not until I know for sure what he's up to. At the elevator, I jab my finger on the down button. Music from the 90s plays overhead, making me wonder when I became old. The doors open before I can ponder this too much and I make my way into the darkness.

It's odd, really. Maurice hated being in the dark when we were kids. Now he thrives in it, a mad scientist in every sense of the word. He's in his lab, which I only know because of the loud music playing overhead.

"*Phantom of the Opera*?" I ask as I stroll in. "Isn't that kind of cliché?"

Maurice's face pales when I enter his lab. He turns his back on me, shaking his bald head.

"You aren't supposed to be in here."

"I need something from you."

I step around piles of junk until I'm on the opposite side of his workbench. He keeps his gaze averted, focused on the tiny creation in his hand.

"Mo, this is important."

He scoffs at that. "It's always important, Ri. My answer is still no."

"It's about the woman I had you look into. She's in danger."

That makes him pause. "Danger?"

"Her father is a bad man. He hurt her. He's going to keep hurting her until I can get her out of there."

"Don't worry about the birdie. Luca has eyes on her," he mutters as he puts on glasses that make his eyeballs look like the size of golf balls.

Maurice has always said shit that makes little sense, but something tells me there's more to it than I know.

Reaching for one of his tools, I ask, "How long has Luca had eyes on her?"

Maurice takes the tool from my hand, putting it back in place. "A while." He looks up. "He wants to put her in a cage so he can watch her forever."

"Fuck."

"That too, I'm sure."

"Mo, I need to know what Luca knows about her."

"Everything."

"Does he know she was with me today?"

Maurice gets a faraway look in his eyes, and I don't think he's going to answer.

"No. He doesn't. But he'll find out and then he'll take her from you. Just like he always does."

"Mo, does he have the room at Grandfather's place ready for her?"

Maurice flinches, but nods. "It was completed just this week."

God damn it. That means Luca is almost ready to make his move.

"Do you know how he found her?"

That makes Maurice laugh, which sounds strange since he doesn't do it often.

"I'd guess the same way you did. Birdies can't seem to stay away from us."

He meets my gaze, and the tortured depth staring back at me makes it hard to breathe. This poor, broken man didn't deserve the hell we were put through as kids. Luca and I couldn't handle it, but Mo never stood a chance.

"Grandfather would be so proud to know that we're still carrying on, even though he's gone." His eyes glaze. "Gone. But never forgotten."

"Mo, I need to know where Luca is."

He doesn't answer, as he hums to himself. This is how he copes with our past. He shuts down and self-soothes by singing or humming. I want to curse but can't. Maurice is this way because of our grandfather, but also because of me and Luca. If escaping into his mind helps him, then I won't try to stop him. Lord knows he's going to need all the peace he can get if Luca has truly prepared the house for Dove.

"It's okay, Mo. I'll figure it out on my own." I say as I leave.

I don't want to deal with Luca, but I'd rather work with him than against him. As much as I hate to admit it, he has resources I don't because I've removed myself from the game.

My chest is tight as I make my way outside. Time to face my demon. Or, in this case, the Beast.

*Luca*

I watch the feeds of the bar, making sure everything is up to par. I spend most nights here, only popping into my hotel when I'm needed. A perk of being on top. When I see a familiar dark head making its way through the crowds, I frown. What in the fuck is he doing here? He knows better than to show his face at any of my establishments.

Pressing the button on my phone, I say, "Don't let my cousin in. Understand?"

"Yes, sir," my secretary answers.

I like her. She's older and doesn't put up with anyone's shit, which means Henri won't be able to charm his way past her. Turning my attention back to my computer, I watch Dove's apartment. She's not back yet, which is odd. She's normally home by now. Maybe she went to get coffee with her boyfriend. The thought has me glaring. I'd be able to check, but she lost the phone with the bug in it, and I haven't been able to slip into her apartment to add one to her new phone. Yet.

"Sir, you can't go in there. Sir!"

The door to my office bursts open, and Henri strolls in as if he has any right to be here, slamming the door in my secretary's face.

"Do you answer your fucking phone?"

Closing my laptop, I reply, "I do."

"Then why in the fuck didn't you answer my calls?"

"I was busy. Some of us work long hours and don't get to go home when the school bell rings."

He glares, and I laugh. It's always been a piece of cake to rile him.

"Make an appointment and come back another time."

He sits in the chair across from my desk, crossing his thick arms. "Not going to fucking happen."

"Don't think that just because we're related, I won't shoot you."

"Taking a page from Grandfather's book? Why am I not surprised?" He looks around. "Is Mo around? Should someone warn him to hide?"

I grip the edge of my desk, so I don't lunge across and knock out his ass.

He notices and laughs. "Showing your emotions, Luca? Now that's something that Grandfather never would have stood for."

"You have three fucking seconds to tell me why you're here."

He loses the cocky glint in his eyes, which is interesting. I don't know if I've ever seen Henri this serious before. Whatever he's going to say is something that I'll be able to use against him, and the thought makes me tremendously happy. In daylight, I deal with money. But secrets are the best currency, and Henri has a big one.

"It seems we have a common interest, and as much as I hate to come to you, I think we need to work together."

"A common interest? I find that hard to believe."

"I'd wager you were just watching our shared interest before I walked in. You have put cameras in her father's apartment, yes?"

His surefire tone makes me pause for a moment. He might be reaching, but he might also know what I've been up to. But wait. He said shared, which means he might be watching her, too. Thoughts of smashing his face into my desk over and over until his brains leak out of his thick head dance through my mind, but I wait. For now.

"Let's say I believe you. You've shown me your hand, and we both know I hold more cards. What's left for you, Henri?"

Another look I can't decipher flashes across his face.

"Her father hurt her."

He's lying. I'd know if something happened to her!

He fucking gloats. "You didn't know? No, how would you? She's been with me all day, which isn't her usual routine."

I want to end him. How dare he imply that he knows more about Dove than me? But that would explain why she's not home yet. Fucking bastard! How did he get to her? I've been so careful.

"We're going to spend the weekend together, though I suspect you're going to make a move before then." He leans forward, gripping the edge of my desk. "I want in."

"In?"

"Mo said you've prepped Grandfather's house, cage, and all. I. Want. In."

Fucking Maurice. He's never been able to keep secrets from Henri. I've never understood their bond. Here it is, screwing me over yet again.

I ask, "And you think she'll want you once she realizes that her life is now in our hands?"

Several emotions flicker across his face, making me chuckle.

"This right there is why Grandfather left me with everything. You and Maurice are too soft to do what needs to be done."

"And you're the heartless beast. His protégé and golden child. I'm well aware, Luca, but I still want in."

I tap my fingers on the desk, thinking. Dove is mine. That much I know. But Henri has something that I want. Something that my grandfather left him because he knew it would piss me off. This might be a win-win situation for me. I get the girl and everything else that should be mine.

"I'll let you in on one exception."

"The muskets?"

I laugh. "God, no. You can keep that morbid reminder of our childhood. I want the ring."

"No."

"Then I guess we have nothing left to talk about. You can see yourself out."

Henri doesn't move, not that I expected him to. He's predictable, one of many flaws he never overcame. He'll give me what I want just as he thinks he can really beat me at a game I've spent my whole life playing.

"What is it with you and the ring? He didn't want you to have it. More importantly, *she* didn't want you to have it, either."

He's talking about my mother, who's only dying wish was that I did not get her ring, and that it be passed on to

Henri's mother. That ring is mine, and everyone knows it. It takes every ounce of willpower I possess not to pull out my gun and shoot him right between the eyes.

"I don't expect you to understand."

He stares at me as if he thinks he can break me. He won't.

Finally, he nods. "You can have the ring if you win Dove."

I don't even bother hiding the grin spreading across my face. "Deal."

We shake hands, just as my phone dings with a notification from the security feed in her house. Since Henri knows my secret, I don't feel bad for opening the feeds on my computer screen. The apartment is tiny, but that didn't stop me from installing multiple cameras in every room. Some might call what I've done an invasion of privacy. I call it monitoring my property.

The little brother bursts through the door first, talking a million miles an hour. He's carrying a box of pizza that he puts on the table before grabbing two plates. Dove enters next, carrying her infant sister's carrier. I can't see her face clearly, so I hit the zoom key. Her hair is down, covering most of her face. When she turns her head, I see the bruises that Henri mentioned.

My fist clenches. "You're sure it was her father?"

"Positive."

Pressing the intercom, I tell my assistant, "Have the pit bosses find David Potts. I'd like a word with him."

"Yes, sir."

Potts is likely at the casino trying to win back his money. Oh, I'll let him win. And then I'm going to rip the fucking carpet from under his feet.

Henri says, "I want to be here when he arrives."

"You removed yourself from the family... *business* years ago. What makes you think you can demand to be here now?"

The Henri I knew years ago would have huffed at my words, exploding in anger. This Henri is different. He leans back in a casual pose that would probably strike fear into the hearts of weaker men. Good thing I'm not weak.

"You don't know?"

"Know what?"

He smirks. "Oh, this is great. I thought for sure someone would have told you by now."

"Tell me what?"

"Come on, Luca. You didn't really think Mo was the one killing all those men, did you?"

His eyes dance with satisfaction that makes me want to punch him. The thing is, I have wondered how my cousin has done my bidding. As my righthand man, it often falls on his shoulders to take care of loose ends. Maurice has never enjoyed killing, but when the bodies turn up in the lake or were never found, I just assumed he was doing what needed to be done.

"So the Brute still lives?"

Henri rolls his eyes. "What was it Grandfather used to say? The Beast was only one-third of the machine. Face it, Luca, you've needed me all along, even if you didn't know it."

"I guess we'll see." I stand. "Let's go hunting."

All doubts about Henri telling the truth leave my mind when I see him shift into killer mode. Grandfather used to say watching Henri turn it on was an art form. In my youth, I never saw it. I understand what he meant now. Henri Gastov is no longer standing before me. No, in his place is the Brute.

"Come, cousin. Let's put this game into action."

My plan was set to go into motion tomorrow, but every good game master knows that you can't control everything and that you have to adapt to the current situation. In fact, this may be the opening I've been looking for. David Potts is a dead man walking, and tonight I put him on notice.

Outside, my car is waiting. My driver, Pierre, looks surprised to see Henri with me, but I shake my head, letting him know that this is fine. We're both silent as we ride to the casino. My word is law around here, so when I said I wanted David Potts found, I know it will be handled by the time I arrive.

At the casino, we enter through a private door. One of my pit bosses waits for me.

"Potts is at the blackjack table."

"How much has he lost tonight?"

"Two thousand."

"How much in total does he owe us?"

"Six."

I nod. "Up the ante. Invite him to a private poker game on the second floor. Give him three orange chips to entice him."

"Will do."

I turn to Henri, motioning for him to follow me to my office.

"How long do you think it will take him to blow through the money?"

I smile. "Not long. I've watched him play. He always thinks he's going to win, and he gets cocky. I'll make sure he wins one hand, and then his ass is mine."

The feeds from the casino floor pop up on several TV screens. My pit boss finds Potts, slapping him on the shoulder with a smile. I see the moment he's told about the private game. He nods, taking the chips. Fool. He's just sealed his fate. Upstairs, the game starts, and, like clockwork, Potts wins the first hand. When he loses the next one, he orders a drink. The second loss has him visibly sweating, but he's still not ready to call it. Not that quitting would save him. Nothing is going to save him.

Lifting the phone on my desk, I dial the game room.

"Offer him a loan of 30k."

"Yes, sir."

The dealer relays my message, and Potts nods. And now he's just signed his death warrant.

Two games later, Potts has lost everything. Two guards stand behind him in case he tries to run. When he says he can't pay, he's led to an elevator.

I stand. "Ready?"

Henri doesn't answer, but follows me to the holding cell. The room is usually used on people who get handsy or with people who try to cheat. Sometimes it's used for moments like this, where someone is about to take their last breath.

When he's shoved into the room, he whimpers.

Henri scoffs. "Already crying? Why am I not surprised?"

I ask Potts, "Do you know who I am?"

"You're the Beast."

I nod. "Good. That will make this a lot easier. You owe me a lot of money, Potts. Money I don't think you have."

"I can get it. I swear!"

I snort. "I've seen your yearly salary, Potts. Don't insult me like that."

"I can sell some things. My daughter has a laptop. That has to be worth something."

I shake my head. "A laptop isn't worth sixty thousand dollars, Potts."

"Please. There has to be something I can do to pay you back. I'll do anything!"

"Anything?"

He nods. "Yes."

"And if I told you to drop to your knees and suck my cock, you would?"

He visibly swallows and lowers to his knees.

I laugh. "Get up. There's no way I'd let you anywhere near my cock. But you do have something that I want. Something I would be willing to forgive your debts for."

"It's yours. Whatever it is, you can have it!"

"I want your daughter. In return, I'll forgive your debts. I'll even give you a little extra to show my thanks."

His throat bobs. "How much extra?"

"Let's say 30K. Does that suit you?"

"Yes. That's more than fair!"

"Good." I pull the check from my breast pocket, handing it to him. "I will collect her tonight at eight. Make sure she knows I'm coming."

He grabs the check, looking it over, before tucking it into his pocket. He's so predictable that it almost takes some of the fun out of the game. Almost.

"If she runs, you're going to pay. Understand?"

"She won't run. You have my word."

Victory courses up my spine as we shake hands.

Turning to Henri, I say, "Now, show Potts just how serious we are."

Henri cracks his knuckles, moving toward Potts.

Potts' eyes widen. "Wha-"

Henri's fist makes satisfying contact with Potts' face. Blood sprays in the air, something I don't think I'll ever tire of seeing. I stand back, watching. Damn. Guess Henri was telling the truth when he said he's the one who's been taking care of my problems. Potts screams fill the air as I turn, lifting my phone, calling Maurice.

"We're going to Grandfather's house tonight."

My entire body feels like electric currents are coursing through it. The game has started. And now it's time for some fun.

# 7

*Dove*

After getting home and feeding Chip and Belle, I dropped the kids off with Mrs. McCarthy so I can have some uninterrupted studying time. My mind is all over the place, though, mostly filled with thoughts of Henri. Good lord. I get all hot and bothered just thinking about everything that we did today. Leaning back in the chair, I close my eyes and remember the way he looked at me. I don't think anyone has ever looked at me like that. It's scary and makes me happy at the same time.

Sighing, I turn my attention back to my notes. I've been studying for an hour when the front door opens and my father stumbles in. His left eye is swollen shut and there are bruises and cuts all over his face and arms. His nose is crooked, as if it's broken. What in the hell happened to him? He glares at me, stumbling into a chair at the table. I can smell the alcohol from here. Did he get in a drunken brawl?

"Stop staring at me and make yourself useful, you cunt. Get me something for my eye!"

I move to the fridge, grabbing a bag of frozen peas. I know from experience that peas feel the best against black eyes. He takes the bag, pressing it against his eye. I'm scared to move. He's in a mood, and there's a chance he might try to take it out on me if I do anything to piss him off. He leans back, the chair groaning in protest. There's a part of me that hopes it breaks under his weight.

"Can I get you anything else?"

He snorts. "You've done enough, but you won't be my problem much longer."

"What does that mean?"

He drops the bag on the table and stands. "It means, you little bitch, that I'm finally getting rid of you. Best say goodbye to your siblings. You won't ever see them again."

His breath reeks of alcohol. I have half a mind to send him to bed. But then he speaks again.

"Got a pretty penny, too. Not sure what a man like Di Bello wants with you, but that's not my problem."

I might have chalked this up to him being drunk, but the moment he mentions Di Bello's name, something tells me he's telling the truth.

"Di Bello? Are you saying you sold me to the mafia?"

"Sure as fuck did. If I had known they were looking for whores, I would have sold you sooner." He reaches into his pocket, pulling out a check. "Thirty thousand, plus he's forgiving all of my debts at the casino."

From here I can see the Di Bello crest. The bloody rose. My throat is tight. This can't be happening. He's going to tell me he's joking any minute now. Why would Di Bello want me? Everything around me dims, and I'm afraid I'm going to pass out.

"They'll be here at eight to collect you." He smiles. "I

don't recommend trying anything stupid until then. I'd hate to send you to him covered in bruises."

"You mean more bruises than I already have?"

His eyes widen, and then he laughs. "I'll let that slide. Now get out of my sight."

I'm already opening my door and entering my room. One of Chip's toys in on the floor and I lift it. My father *sold* me. What kind of person does that? And who's saying he won't do it to Chip or Belle? I don't want to think about the kind of person who would buy another person, much less a child. Which means my options are clear. I have to get out of here and make sure nothing happens to my siblings. Something I should have done a long time ago.

Glancing at my phone, I look at the time. It's almost seven, which means I have an hour to pull this off. My father will not let me just walk out of the door, so I need to be smart. My gaze goes to the fire escape. I can take it down a floor and take the stairs back to our floor. Better yet, maybe Mrs. McCarthy can meet me downstairs. I send her a text and she responds right away, saying she'll meet me.

Digging under my mattress, I pull out the lockbox with money that I've been stashing. There's nearly five thousand, but I know it won't last us long.

"Think, Dove. You need a place to stay tonight."

Henri's face crosses my mind. I text him.

**Me: Does your offer still stand? For me and my siblings?**

**Me: It's kind of an emergency.**

**Me: Please text me when you get this.**

Hopefully, he'll come through for me. If not, I'll be using some of my precious cash for a motel room. It won't be the end of the world, but I'd rather not waste the money if I can avoid it. My father laughs from the living room, reminding me that time is literally slipping away. Quietly, I grab clothes for Chip and Belle, stuffing them into a bag. I also pack as many diapers as I can find, knowing they are going to be what I need the most. That and formula. I'm so thankful that I brought the formula with me last night. Now it's one less thing I have to worry about right now. I turn my attention to my belongings.

My laptop and schoolbooks are first. Then some clothes. Last is the small paper box that contains a necklace that my mom left for me, at least that's what my father said. He could have been lying, but I'd like to think she left something of hers behind for me. Looking around the room, I realize that this is it. The moment I've been waiting for. The day my life begins. So why am I so scared?

One of Belle's toys is in her crib, and I lift it, letting the sweet scent that can only be found on a baby fill my nose. Am I doing the right thing for them? Their future isn't guaranteed to be safe and easy with me. The only thing I can promise is that I'll do the best that I can. And I will never hurt them. If they stay, my father *will* hurt them. I know that. I take a deep breath and shove the toy in my bag.

It's now or never.

The window lifts easily, and I step onto the rickety fire escape. The metal groans as I make my way down one flight of stairs to the maintenance entry. Mrs. McCarthy is waiting with Chip and Belle. Her eyes are wide with worry as she helps me in.

"Is there anything I can do?"

I take her arm. "You've done so much. I'll never be able to thank you enough."

"Please be safe."

"I will."

She gives me the carrier. I'm happy to see that Belle is

asleep. That will make things easier. Chip is bouncing on his heels next to me.

"Mrs. McCarthy said we're going on a trip. Is Dad coming?"

She gives me a sympathetic smile as I lower to my knees.

"No, buddy. It's just going to be the three of us. Is that okay?"

He ponders this for a moment. "Yeah. I don't like it when Dad yells. He's not mad at us, is he?"

I lie, "No. In fact, he's excited for us."

"Where are we going?"

I still haven't felt my phone buzz, so I answer, "A motel for tonight. Tomorrow, we'll figure out where we want to go."

"Is there a pool at the motel?"

"Probably."

"Cool!"

I stand, facing Mrs. McCarthy. "Thank you again."

"If you're going to a motel, I know someone who works at Hôtel de Lumière. I'm sure she won't mind giving you a discount."

"Oh my goodness. That would be amazing. Are you sure it's not a problem?"

"No problem at all. It's the least I can do."

She pulls out her phone and calls someone. I try not to listen, but from what I can gather, it sounds like her friend will give us a discount. I've passed by Hôtel de Lumière before, but never dreamed of stepping inside. Mostly because it's so fancy and it intimidates me. But this might be what I need. If someone in the Di Bello Family truly did buy me from my father, then they won't expect me to be right under their nose in a hotel they own. That's what I'm counting on at least.

"You can have the room for a hundred dollars. Ask for Angela and you must pay in cash."

I exhale loudly. "Thank you so much, Mrs. McCarthy."

"It's my pleasure. Now go. And once you're settled, be sure to send word that you're safe. I'll worry about the three of you until then."

We hug, and I try my hardest not to cry. I don't want to worry Chip, who is watching the interaction between the two of us.

"Thank you." To Chip I say, "Come on, buddy."

"Dove, why are you sad?"

"I'm not sad. I'm just excited."

"You're crying because you're excited?"

I smile. "Yeah. We're going to stay in a nice hotel and then tomorrow we're going to take a bus ride somewhere fun."

"To Oklahoma?"

My eyebrows lift. "Why Oklahoma?"

"We learned about it in school. There was a thing there called a land run. Can we do that?"

"I'm not sure if things still work like that, but we can go to Oklahoma if that's where you want to go."

"It is!"

"Once we get to the hotel, I'll see if there's a bus going to Oklahoma then."

Because I'm sure my father won't think to look for us there. He'll start out in places where we have family, which is out west. The south won't be on his radar, which makes it perfect. I lead the way down the stairs to the first floor and order an Uber. The car arrives a moment later and we get in. My nerves are all over the place. What if my father was talking out of his head? What if we get caught, and they say I'm kidnapping Chip and Belle? What if—

"Hey, lady. We're here."

"Oh. Thanks."

Hôtel de Lumière is one of the most expensive hotels in the world. I know this because I watched a documentary on it. It rises high into the sky, and each room offers a view of the city or the lake. It's been in the Di Bello family for a long time, but didn't become successful until Luca Di Bello took over in 2001. I was one year old. That's why I can't figure out why anyone in the Di Bello family would want to buy me. I'm nothing to them, and they've all got to be so much older.

The exterior of the hotel is a golden color. It's your first glance at the wealth and decadence that lies within the massive golden doors. Two men in royal purple bellhop outfits stand on each side of the doors and open them when we approach. The marbled tile floor is white with streaks of gold that catch the light from the massive chandelier. There're pops of gold and royal purple everywhere, but the thing that surprises me most are the gold candelabras with real wax candles burning in them. You just don't see that anymore, probably because it's a massive fire danger.

"Can I help you?" A man asks, while sniffing the air as if something smells foul. Prick.

"I'm looking for Angela."

"She will be out shortly. You may wait over there."

He gestures to a corner behind a large potted plant. Out of sight, out of mind, I guess.

"Come on, Chip," I mutter.

"Dove, that man scares me. He looks like he eats kids for breakfast."

I mean, he's kind of right. Outside, rain falls from the sky and a chilly breeze moves through the lobby when a man arrives. I shiver. It feels like an omen. What if this is a mistake? What if I was wrong, and being here put me right in the line of fire? I'm about ready to leave when an older woman walks toward me.

"I'm Angela. Are you Dove?"

"I am. Thanks again for doing this."

She waves her hand. "It's no problem. Now, do you have the cash?"

Reaching into my pocket, I pull out the money and hand it to her. She tucks it into her jacket and hands me a plastic keycard.

"You're in room 711. The elevators are to the left. Try not to let anyone see you. I could get into a lot of trouble for selling you the room at such a discounted rate."

I take the key before she changes her mind. "Thanks. We'll be gone in the morning."

She smiles at me and then darts away. Her nervous energy is contagious, and I grip the baby carrier and lead Chip toward the elevator.

A man stands inside and asks, "Which floor, ma'am?"

"Seven."

The cart lifts and the man stares straight ahead as if we're not even there. When we reach the seventh floor, we step onto plush carpet that my shoes sink into and follow the signs for our room. Chip lets out an excited squeal when I open the door. The room is bigger than our apartment and much nicer. Chip darts in and jumps onto the nearest bed.

"Can we stay here forever?"

"Just tonight, bud."

Because I looked up the usual nightly rate for a room here. Angela gave us a five-hundred-dollar discount. I can't imagine ever paying that much for a room for one night! Chip grabs the remote for the TV and turns it on while I take Belle out of her carrier, putting her on my bed. She's still sleeping, so I cover her with a blanket before looking in her diaper bag. There's less than a can of formula between what I grabbed from the apartment and what was in her bag, which means I will need to buy more before we leave town.

After a quick internet search, I discover that there's a grocery store near the bus station. Perfect. I can get formula and snacks for our trip. Next, I look at bus tickets. I wish there was a train to Oklahoma, but I'd have to go all the way to New Orleans and then go from there, which is out of the way. The bus trip is going to take over eighteen hours, and that's if the bus is on time. I groan, wishing I could find a quicker solution. Both kids are going to be miserable by the time we get there. Maybe I should break the trip up? Go somewhere closer before going to Oklahoma.

After searching, I decide that the cheapest route is to go straight to Oklahoma. Once we get there, I'll look into a place to stay. The cost of living is cheap, so hopefully my money will go further than it will here.

Chip asks, "Can we go swimming?"

"I think the pool is closed for the night. Want to take a bubble bath?"

"Yeah!" He darts into the bathroom and calls out, "Holy cow! I think there is a pool in here, Dove!"

I follow him and laugh when I see him standing in the tub. It's not a pool by any means, but is larger than the one back home.

"Let me fill up the tub while you get undressed."

He climbs out, and I get to work filling the tub. Once it's halfway full, I let him get back in and turn on the jets. He leans back, sighing, as if this is the happiest he's ever been. My heart pulls. Maybe it is. He's old enough to realize that we aren't like other families. Maybe he's old enough to see how much we've been struggling.

"Dove, are crying because you're happy again?"

I nod, wiping at my eyes. "I am. I'm just super excited that we're going on a trip. Our bus leaves at nine tomorrow morning, so we're going to have to get up early so we can go to the store and get some snacks."

"Snacks?" His eyes light up. "Like gummy bears?"

"Sure, if that's what you want. And I was thinking we can get some stuff to make peanut butter and jelly sandwiches, too."

"And chips," he adds with a toothy grin.

"Definitely can't forget the chips."

I let him play in the tub while I make a list of everything to get at the store. By the time Chip gets out, Belle is awake, and crying for a bottle. She gurgles happily at me as I feed her. I'm so worried that this trip is going to be too much for them. We have to change buses twice. What if we miss one? Groaning, I close my eyes. When I open them, the clock on the wall chimes eight. Nervous energy fires through me. If my father was telling the truth, then Di Bello's men will arrive at the apartment, looking for me.

Several scenarios cross my mind. Will they hurt my father, wanting to know where I am? Will he even notice I'm gone? Is it possible that they will track me? I paid cash for everything, but there are traffic cameras everywhere. I stand, needing to move. Coming here seemed like a good idea at first, but what if I was wrong? What if I've walked right into the den of the beast?

There's nothing I can do now except wait and see. When Belle is done eating, I reach for my phone. Still nothing from Henri, which hurts. Maybe he had time to rethink what we did and decided it wasn't a good idea. He is, after all, my professor. I'm sure he'd get in trouble if anyone ever found out what we had done. My face warms at the thought.

At least I'll have those memories to carry me on. I doubt I'll ever feel safe enough to let someone get that close to me ever again.

Once the kids are asleep, I lay out everything I packed plus what was in their bags at Mrs. McCarthy and then repack everything so it's not so bulky. I pack all the diapers in the diaper bag, as well as a few changes of clothes for Belle, in case she has an accident. In Chip's backpack, I pack some of his favorite toys and leave room for snacks.

My schoolbooks stare back at me. It seems kind of silly to have brought them. I won't be able to do the work remotely. After I miss five consecutive days, the school will consider me delinquent, and my standing will be put on hold. I decide to email the dean, saying that there has been an emergency and that I need to drop all of my courses for the rest of the year. This way I don't lose all the work I've put in. With any luck, I will pick up where I left off. One of these days...

I push my schoolbooks to the side. There's no need to bring them, but I do pack my laptop. Nine o'clock comes and goes. So does ten. By eleven, I'm struggling to keep my eyes open. I know I should go to bed, but there's a feeling deep in the pit of my stomach warning me that something bad is coming and that I need to be ready to run. I check the bags again and then I peek at Chip and Belle, who are both soundly sleeping.

"You're being ridiculous, Dove," I mutter.

There's a loud knock on the front door. Dread coils through my body. Who could it be? I reach the door, peering through the peephole. The man from the front desk is there, and Angela is at his side. *Oh no*.

"Ma'am, we can see your shadow. Please open the door or I will be forced to call the authorities."

Cursing under my breath, I open the door. Angela's eyes are red, as if she's been crying. Great. This isn't looking good.

"Ma'am, I was told that you paid cash for a room tonight. Is that correct?"

I nod, not wanting to lie.

"I'm sorry to say that unless you can pay the rest of the cost of the room, then I'm going to have to ask that you leave."

"I can pay the rest."

"Excellent. That will be twelve hundred dollars."

My mouth drops. "But the website said the rate is six hundred a night."

"It usually is, but there's an event at the hotel the next few days, and the rates are higher." He eyes me. "Is that going to be a problem?"

"No. I just need to get my purse."

He nods, sniffing the air. "We'll wait."

Closing the door, I lean against it for a moment. Twelve hundred dollars! That's going to cut into my money stash a lot. If I don't pay, then we're going to be out on the streets until the bus station opens. My eyes water. I'll just pay it and then be extra careful with the rest. Padding across the floor, I grab my purse. When I open the door, the man is in the middle of chastising Angela, who is crying again.

"Here."

He looks appalled. "I can't take your money. You will have to come to the front desk and check in as every other guest does. You'll need identification, too."

I bite the inside of my cheek. "My little sister and brother are asleep in there. Can I do it in the morning?"

"No."

Angela chooses this moment to speak up. "I can stay with them while you go downstairs."

I glare. *Now* she wants to play by the rules?

"Let me grab my wallet."

Angela follows me into the room and whispers, "I'm so sorry. He saw you getting on the elevators and started asking questions. I was afraid I was going to lose my job."

"I'm the one who should apologize! You were just doing me a huge favor when you didn't have to."

She gives me a weak smile. "Once you pay, everything will be okay."

She sits in the chair by the window, scrolling on her phone. I'm not thrilled about leaving a stranger with my siblings, but I'll only be gone for a few minutes. In the hallway, Mr. Prick leads the way to the elevator, never speaking. In the lobby, he takes me to an office, where he slides over a form for me to fill out.

"I need a copy of a government issued ID or passport."

I slide my license and then fill out the paperwork. I thought most places like this were all electronic, but maybe I'm wrong. Maybe it's part of the whole old-world vibe. I'm almost finished when the phone on the desk rings. The man answers the phone, nodding. His gaze goes to my license as he whispers into the receiver. The walls feel like they're closing in on me. Did he just say my name or am I imagining things?

Finally, he ends the call and says, "I'm going to make a copy of this. I'll be right back."

It's on the tip of my tongue to tell him I've changed my mind, but that might draw more attention. So, I wait, tapping my foot to let out the nervous energy coursing through me.

The door opens and Mr. Prick enters. But he's not alone.

A massive man stands behind him, arms crossed over his chest. And the thing I notice second? The tattoo on his hand. The Di Bello crest.

"Miss. Potts, I'm going to have to ask that you go quietly with this man."

"Wh-who is he?"

"He works with the Di Bello Family. You have something that they want."

I shake my head. "I have nothing. There's been some kind of misunderstanding."

"If that is the case, then I'm sure Mr. Di Bello will let you go as soon as you tell him." His tone suggests that he doesn't believe me.

Hot tears fill my eyes and there's a sharp burning sensation in the back of my nose. I won't cry. I won't! My options zoom through my mind, all fleeing just as quickly. I could try to run, but the massive man blocking the doorway will probably stop me in my tracks. I could scream, but who will believe my word against a Di Bello? I could go, but there's no telling what will happen if I do. The thing is, I know the Di Bello Family runs part of the city. If they want me, they're going to get me. No matter what.

"What about my siblings?"

"We will watch them until you return."

His words give me an odd sense of courage, like I'll be back sooner than later.

"I'd like my ID back, please."

He hands it to me, and I tuck it into my wallet before turning to the man.

"I'm ready."

# 8

### Di Bello

*Dove*

I'm led outside to a waiting car. The man holds an umbrella over my head, so I don't get wet, but that doesn't stop me from shivering. The streets are empty as I climb inside. The leather seats are heated, but I'm still cold. When the car pulls away from the hotel, I whimper. I can't see anything through the tinted windows. The man driving meets my gaze in the mirror before glancing away. Does he know that Di Bello has bought me? Would he help me if I asked?

I'm about to open my mouth when the partition lifts, cutting us off. Now I feel more alone than before. Not only that, but I'm now sitting in complete darkness, which leaves me with my thoughts. Where are we going? Are Chip and Belle okay? What's going to happen to them if my father was telling the truth? Will they be sent back to him? Hot tears fill my eyes. I won't cry. If I do, then I might not stop, and I need to keep my wits about me. That doesn't stop the bile from creeping up my throat. I haven't eaten all day, but that doesn't stop me from wanting to vomit right now. Wonder what Di Bello would do if I barfed all over his nice car? A nervous laugh escapes.

I'm not sure how long we drive. Could be a few moments, but I think it's longer. By the time the car comes to a stop, my entire body is trembling. My door opens and I find another man standing there holding an umbrella.

"Where am I?"

I hate that my voice cracks.

He doesn't answer and nods his head toward the imposing mansion.

"I'm not going in there."

He gives my shoulder a little shove, knocking me forward. When I glace back at him, he has a stubborn set to his jaw. If I don't walk on my own, he's going to make me. So, I walk. My mind is going a million miles an hour as I climb the steps to the house. It's hard to believe we're still in Chicago. This house and the ground it sits on remind me of something right out of France.

I reach the door and stop. Do I just go in or...?

There's another shove to my back.

"Jeez. I get it. I'm going in. You don't have to keep shoving me," I say as I push open the door.

It creaks, like every horror movie I've ever seen, and I want to run. But the goon behind me is close enough that I can feel the heat coming off his body. Good. Maybe he'll die first. Slowly, I move into the foyer. It's massive, as if someone wants to show off their wealth. Black marble floors, black walls, iron railings on the stairs that lead upward toward darkness. There're two doors on each side of the stairway. I feel that either option leads to certain death.

The man grunts, nodding toward one door.

"Are you coming with me?"

He shakes his head. Well, crap. Inhaling, I move toward

the door. Entering, I find myself in an enormous library that spans two stories. Holy heck. Moving inward, I try to take in everything around me. There have to be millions of books! The scent of leather and cigar smoke lingers in the air, making me think that I'm not alone. I should be scared, but I'm drawn to the stained-glass window. It's gruesome, but somehow beautiful at the same time. A beast runs through a field as an arrow pierces its side. Blood sprays, represented with red glass that catches the light outside.

"My grandfather loved that piece. Had it drawn up after a dream he had."

Turning, I try to find the source of the voice. Footsteps move above me, and the hairs on the back of my neck stand as the steps echo down the stairs.

"Why am I here?" I call out. "I'm pretty sure kidnapping is illegal."

He chuckles, and I know he's close. "It's only kidnapping if someone reports you as missing."

Fear creeps up my throat, making it hard to breathe. I mean, he's not wrong.

"Why am I here?" I ask again.

A man steps from the shadows, and my hand goes over my mouth. He's taller than me and wears all black. But what has me taking a step back is the mask he wears over his face. All I can see are dark eyes and his lips, which are lifting, as if he's smiling. But that mask... I'd know it anywhere. Hell, *everyone* in Chicago knows who the mask belongs to and what it means.

"You know who I am?"

"You're the Beast. The head of the Di Bello Family."

The wooden mask is carved to look like a terrifying beast, and it works. I've heard urban legends all my life about this mask. That people only see it when they're going to die. Is that what's about to happen to me?

"Very good," he purrs. "I was worried you wouldn't know who I was, which would complicate things."

I take another step back. "I have done nothing to warrant a meeting with you."

"Haven't you?" He takes a step toward me. "I know you've sensed me over the last few weeks."

I swallow and find myself pressed against a bookshelf behind me. He moves until I'm caged in. My gaze darts around, trying to find an escape. I have to get away from him, I know that much.

He presses his hand over my breast. "I can feel your heart pounding. Tell me, little bird, is it out of fear or desire?"

His words stun me before pissing me off.

"It's not desire!"

He chuckles darkly. "No, I don't suppose it would be out of desire yet."

Yet? Yet! I shake my head, denying him. I will *never* desire him!

"I want to go home."

"You are home."

"No, I'm not. My home is on the other side of town. Just have your goon take me back. I swear I won't call the cops or anything."

He can't see the hand behind my back, nor does he know I'm crossing my fingers.

"You *are* home, Dove."

He says it as if it's the truth.

"No, I'm not. I want to go."

I try to move past him, but he stops me with one muscular arm.

"You are home."

"You're crazy."

He snorts. "I've been called worse. That doesn't change the fact that this is now your home. I suggest you come to terms with it sooner than later. I did, after all, pay a lot of money for you."

Guess dear old dad was telling the truth about selling me. Fucking jerk!

"What happens if I don't come to terms with it?"

His gaze narrows. "You don't want to find out."

The realization that I should have run a long time ago hits me like a ton of bricks. He's been watching me for months and I ignored my gut feeling that told me to run. And now I'm trapped in his house. A whimper escapes my mouth before I can stop it.

He sighs. "It's always the hard way."

Before I can ask what he means, he scoops me up, tossing me over his shoulder like I don't weigh two-hundred and fifty pounds. If I wasn't fucking terrified, I'd be impressed. We're out of the library by the time it crosses my mind to fight back.

"Help!" I scream. "I'm being kidnapped! Fire!"

He snorts. "Fire? That's a new one. And no one is going to run and save you unless I tell them to, so you're quite literally wasting your breath."

He climbs the stairway, going to the second floor. I don't thrash while we're on the stairs because I don't want him to drop me. On the second floor, I resume my struggle, which makes him laugh.

"This isn't funny, you psycho! Let me go."

We enter a room bathed in darkness. He tosses me down, and it takes a moment for it to register to my brain that I'm on a bed. Scrambling to a sitting position, I look around the room, trying to get my bearings.

"I'm going to give you some time to cool down and be reasonable."

"Wait!"

The door closes and I hear the unmistakable sound of a door locking. Feeling my way across the room, I find the door and try it. It doesn't budge. Running my hand down the wall, I hope and pray that I find a light switch. When I do, I make an excited sound only for it to fall from my lips. The room is bare, except for a bed and a tin bucket sitting in the room's corner. That better not be for what I think it's for. My gut says it is. There's a window, and that gives me hope until I see the nails in it.

A blinking light in the room's corner near the ceiling catches my eye. So, the Beast is watching me? I hold up both middle fingers to the camera. He thinks he's going to wait until I'm calm and reasonable? Well, he's going to be waiting for a long-fucking-time.

I pace the room for what feels like hours. My stomach grumbles angrily, but I've been hungry before. My anger wavers and is replaced by fear for Chip and Belle. Where are they? Did they get sent back to my father? I almost wish the Beast would come back just so I can ask. But that doesn't happen. So I pace until my head throbs. I don't want to go to sleep. There's no telling what that monster will do to me if I do. But exhaustion finally takes over. Grabbing the pillow and blanket from the bed, I curl up in a corner and close my eyes.

I'm jarred awake when the door opens and a tray of food slides across the floor. The door closes before I can get a word out. The scent of eggs and bacon fill the air, and my stomach growls happily. Too bad I will not eat it. I do drink the water that's on the tray. I'm not stupid—I need water to live. Just so I don't tempt myself, I go back to my corner and cover my head with the pillow, telling myself that I can do this.

The next time I wake up, the tray is gone. In its place is a banana. God, I want to eat it so bad. Holding it up to the camera, I squeeze it until the innards pop out and then throw it against the wall.

"I'm not eating your food," I call out to the empty room. "And you can't make me."

The thing is, I know there are ways he can make me eat if he wants. I just hope it doesn't come to that.

"I need to know where Chip and Belle are. Are they okay?"

Talking out loud makes me feel better, which is an odd discovery. Maybe it's because it lets me know that I'm not alone. That I'm still here, alive and kicking. I sit on the bed this time, looking right at the camera.

"This is really messed up. You have to realize that. I mean, who *buys* a person? And why me? I'm no one special." I sigh. "Please let me know if Chip and Belle are okay. That's all that I ask."

Nothing happens. But several hours later, another food tray is shoved into the room. I glimpse the person. They're wearing a black ski mask, so I can't see their face. Judging by their height and build, it's a man. What kind of person is okay with what's happening to me? I guess it's possible they didn't have a choice. Sighing, I take the water bottle from the tray and go to my corner where I pretend that I'm drinking wine and dining on steak. The same steak that's tempting me from across the room.

The next day starts similarly. Only this time, I finally have to use the bucket in the corner to relieve my bladder. I keep the blanket wrapped around me, glaring at the camera the entire time.

"This is degrading. At least give me toilet paper!"

My food tray comes a bit later. On top sits a roll of toilet paper. So they can hear me? I'm so angry that I throw the tray against the wall. There's nothing breakable on it, but it still makes a mess. Grabbing the water bottle, I go to my corner, facing the wall. Hot tears fall down my face, but I'm not about to let the Beast know that he's getting to me.

Time drags on until the door opens and another tray slides my way. I wonder how long they're going to keep doing this? Eventually, someone is going to have to come and clean in here. Right?

I think I'm handling everything well until the lights go out. Sitting in the dark makes everything feel more ominous. Something scrapes the wall near me, and I jump, whimpering.

"It's nothing," I try to tell myself.

But it doesn't feel like nothing. By the time the lights come back on, I'm openly crying. My relief doesn't last long, though, because the lights flicker once before going out. I try to tell myself that it could be the wiring. This is an old house, and things like that happen. But the little red light on the camera continues to flash. Taunting me. Reminding me that my life is no longer my own. I crawl to the corner, wrapping the blanket around myself. I can survive this. I have to.

Time loses meaning. Trays come with food that I refuse to eat, and the lights are off more often than on. The day that I can't bring myself to move when the door opens is the first time that I wonder if this is what the Beast had planned all along. To break me one day at a time. That makes me grit my teeth. I'll show him. Eventually, he'll be back. And when he does, he's going to regret the day that he took me.

*Luca*

Henri paces the room, making me want to scream. I don't. I would never show an outburst of emotion like that.

"It's been four days. How much longer can she go without eating?"

Maurice, who's tinkering with something in the corner, answers, "A human can go three weeks without food as long as they're drinking enough water."

"There you go."

Henri glares. "I don't like this."

"We need her ready."

He has nothing to say to that because he knows I'm right. She's been sleeping more and more, likely to curb the hunger pains. What she doesn't know is she's putting herself at a disadvantage by refusing to eat. She's going to be weak when the time comes, and it will be her fault. I'll make sure she's aware of this, too. But not today. No, I'm going to give her some more time to think about what she wants.

Henri asks, "How are the kids doing?"

Dove running the other night was the best thing that could have happened. We didn't have to get the boy and infant from their father. No, all I had to do was walk into my hotel with a nanny and take them back to one of my homes.

"They're settling in. The boy has stopped asking where she is."

Maurice clicks his tongue against the roof of his mouth.

"Poor lambs are always lost without the soft hands who take care of them. Good thing they forget. Most of the time."

Henri meets my gaze, and I shake my head. Now is not the time. Maurice will only get worse before he gets better. That's how it's always been.

I say to Henri, "They will be fine. I'll make sure they're taken care of after."

He nods, still looking as if there's something on his mind. I turn my attention back to the camera. The lights are on, and Dove uses the time to go to the bucket in the room's corner. I've never enjoyed watching anyone go to the bathroom, but I find myself drawn to her and what she's doing at all times. Even now, when I should be repulsed. The familiar zing shoots down my spine. I'm going to break her. By the time I'm finished, she won't know who she used to be.

All I need is time.

# 9

*Dove*

*I want to go home. I want to go home. I want to go home.*

I trace the words over and over on the wooden plane of the wall, willing them to be true. I never thought I would miss that place in a million years. At least I knew what to expect from my father. Most of the time, he was happy to leave us alone. My eyes water. Where are Chip and Belle? It's been days. Maybe even weeks. No, not weeks. I don't think I'd be alive if it was weeks. I glance at the food tray. I'm not hungry anymore. What does that mean?

Closing my eyes, I let my thoughts wander. Does anyone know I'm gone? Does Henri? It's strange. I've thought about him a lot while I've been in here. Has he wondered where I've been or did the dean tell him about the email I sent? In retrospect, that was a bad idea. Now no one will look too much into why I've vanished. I groan. Look at me... helping my captor without even meaning to. That's the luck I have.

More time passes, and with it a bit of my sanity. I wonder if I'll go to heaven or hell when I die. I've never been a religious person, but I'd like to think I've been a good person overall. Is that enough to get past the pearly gates? I wonder if I'll finally get to meet my mother. That would be my luck.

Rolling to the side, I look up at the flashing light on the camera. Did the Beast really capture me just to keep me locked in a room until I lost my mind? My gut says no. Which means there's something coming. Something bad. Bad for me. I groan. And I've been refusing food like a dummy. I won't be able to fight him off when he comes back. As if I've summoned him, the door opens, and he stands in the doorway wearing all black and his stupid wooden mask. How did I know that he would arrive just as I thought I was losing my mind?

"I hear you aren't eating."

I grunt, not bothering to answer.

"You're a smart girl, Dove, but this isn't very smart."

I force myself into a sitting position, sending a wave of dizziness through my head.

"I want to leave."

"Okay."

He says the word so casually that I have to ask, "What?"

"I said okay. You can leave." There's a pause. "But not until you eat. Understand?"

His deep voice is soothing, a far cry from how he spoke to me the other day.

"Fine."

"I'll send someone up to take you to the bathroom so you can clean up."

He's gone before I think to ask where Chip and Belle are. Some sister I am. I close my eyes, letting myself doze. I'm just so very tired... A knock on the door startles me. A man wearing a plague mask stands there, making me realize that I'm still surrounded by crazy people.

"Time for your bath, birdie. Better hurry before the Beast changes his mind."

He motions for me to follow him. Fueled by the promise that I will get to leave, I trail behind him. He leads me down a dark hallway, stopping in front of a door.

"Bathroom for the birdie. Don't try anything flighty, or I'll break your wings."

I'm not about to argue with someone wearing a plague mask, so slip into the bathroom, closing the door behind me. There's no lock, but I'm not surprised. The bathroom is minimal, with a shower, sink, and toilet. There's not even a mirror. Guess the Beast is afraid I might take the easy way out and break the glass so I can slit my wrists. On the counter is a toothbrush, a towel, and a long red maxi dress. A quick glance at the tag confirms it's my size. I really don't want to wear a dress, but my clothes smell so bad that I know I don't have a choice.

Grumbling, I undress. Midway, I pause. There's a camera blinking in the shower's corner.

"You're a creep," I mutter as I turn on the water.

When it's warm, I take the fastest shower I've ever taken in my life. I want to stand under the hot spray and let it wash away everything that's happened since I've been here, but I don't. Toweling off, I slip on the maxi dress. The jerk could have at least got me undergarments. Something tells me it wasn't an oversight.

"Perv!"

There's no brush, so I run my fingers through my dark locks, trying to untangle them. Brushing my teeth feels like heaven on earth, even though I don't have toothpaste. I make do, just like I always have. Inhaling, I open the door. The man is standing there as if he's waiting for me.

"I'm ready."

"This way."

I fall in step behind him as I'm led down winding hallways that are likely meant to make it impossible to know where I'm going. Finally, we reach the stairway and make our way to the first floor. At the bottom stands the Beast, but there's a man next to him wearing a wooden mask that looks like the devil. Fitting. These men are the devil.

Beast says, "Look how nicely our guest cleans up. Let's go to the dining room."

I follow the man in the devil's mask. We reach a large dining room with only one place set. The devil pulls out the chair, motioning for me to sit. My pulse skitters.

"Why aren't there other places set?"

Beast answers, "We've already had our meals. Now sit."

I do, because I need answers, and this is probably the best way to get them. Once I'm seated, they take their seats. Beast sits at the head of the table. To his right is the man in the devil's mask and then the man in the plague mask. I sit alone on my side of the table. I try not to let them see my nerves, but it's hard. My foot bounces under the table because I need to get this energy out in some form or fashion.

A woman enters. She's oddly normal compared to the men wearing the masks. If she thinks their attire is odd, she doesn't let it show. No, she walks in and places a bowl of soup in front of me.

"Thank you."

She doesn't answer and leaves out the same door that she came through. I stare at my soup. Is it safe to eat?

"Eat."

"I'll eat once you tell me where Chip and Belle are."

"You'll eat and then I might consider answering you."

Jerk. Reaching for the spoon, I dip it into the soup and

take a small bite. It's flavorful and my stomach rumbles loud enough that I'm sure they hear it. Even if it is poisoned, at least it tastes good.

Beast says, "You made me quite angry by refusing to eat. To me, your actions are childish. My cousin over here thinks you were brave. And my other cousin thinks you were scared. So, little bird, which is it?"

I glance at the Beast. "You're all wrong, but also right. Was it childish? Yes. Am I scared? Yes. Brave? Sometimes. But I didn't eat because I wanted to prove a point."

"And what point is that?"

"I'm not some toy that can be bought and told what to do."

He hums under his breath. "A toy? No, you're not a toy. You're a pet."

My throat is dry, so I reach for my water before I answer, "I'm not a pet, either."

"Aren't you? You've shown all the traits of a pet. Refused to eat because you were scared, but the moment you're led to food, you eat. You hid from me until I said I would free you. Tell me again, little bird, that you aren't a pet."

"I want to go home."

He sighs. "You are home. Eat."

My stomach is protesting, but I finish the soup. Beast nods his head in what I assume is approval when I set down my spoon.

"I'd like to leave now. And I want to know where Chip and Belle are."

"Your siblings are safe. That's all that matters, yes? As for leaving, I think you and I should have a chat before you go."

He stands, and so do the other men. Biting back a shitty comment, I follow them to a formal living room. There's a roaring fire in the fireplace, but that's the only warm thing in this room. The décor reminds me of what you'd expect at a palace—stuffy and uninviting. Definitely not somewhere I'd kick back and relax. And the thought of kids being in this room is laughable. I sit on a chair that is so uncomfortable that I almost consider sitting on the floor instead. The others do the same.

"You wanted to talk?"

"I do." Beast rubs his hands together. "Forgive me. It's been a while since I've had to have this speech with someone. I want to enjoy it."

The devil sighs. "Get to the point, Beast."

His voice does something to my memory, as if I've heard him speak before, which is crazy. Right?

"Brute, you are supposed to be silent," Beast snaps.

Tension is so thick in the room that you could cut it with a knife. My gaze goes between the two men.

I say to the third man, "If you're the Beast and he's the Brute, then what does that make you?"

"I'm the Brain."

"Interesting. Did the three of you name yourselves?"

They don't answer, making me think that maybe they did.

"Listen, I know my father said that he sold me to the Di Bello Family, which I'm guessing means to the Beast, but there's been a mistake."

Beast snorts. "The only mistake is allowing you to stay with him as long as I did. I should have plucked you as soon as I first saw you, but I needed time…"

His voice trails off, and I don't like it.

"Why did you need time? And how long have you been watching me?"

"Long enough."

Is he the reason the hairs on the back of my neck have

been standing whenever I'm out? That's been going on for *months*. My stomach heaves and I fear I'm going to be sick.

"Why me?"

"Ah, now that's a good question." He pauses. "You have a quality within that called to me the moment I laid eyes on you. You're someone I've been looking for. For years."

Brain echoes, "Years."

I shake my head. "This is a mistake. I've done nothing to *call* to you. I'm a nobody, and I certainly didn't ask to be sold to you."

Beast sighs. "I don't expect you to understand. Not yet, at least. Now, let's get back on topic, shall we? As the Brute said, I need to get to the point so that the fun can begin."

"Why do I get the feeling I won't think this is fun?"

He chuckles. "Very good, pet. You're learning."

His tone raises my hackles, but I don't want to let him know he's getting to me. So, I look away. Brute, who sits across from me, is gripping the arms of his chair so tight that his knuckles are white. Does he not agree with what's about to be said? That probably doesn't bode well for me.

"You've been sold to the Di Bello Family, which makes you our property until you die. It's the way things have been done since our family left Italy, and it's the way things will continue to go until the end of time."

My mouth gapes. "Are you serious? How can you say that like it's not wrong?"

He ignores me. "Unlike our forefathers, we have decided to give you a chance to gain your freedom. If you win, you will receive not only your life back, but money to ensure that you and your siblings are taken care of for the rest of your life. Your father will be dealt with, and you won't have to fear him."

"That sounds too good to be true." But then I ask, "What do I have to do to win?"

I hear the smile in his voice as he says, "You will be taken outside. Once the timer starts, all you have to do is reach the red light at the end of the property."

"That seems too simple."

"Ah. Such a smart pet. The property is fifty acres and unkempt. You will fight the elements in nothing more than you have on right now."

"But it's going to be freezing out there. I won't make it in this dress."

His shoulder lifts. "Then I suggest you run as fast as you can. Run like your life depends on it."

He's giving me a warning; I can feel it.

"What happens if I'm caught?"

"My cousins and I will each take part in the chase. What happens to you after is left to our discretion. Myself, I plan on keeping you as a pet until I tire of you."

My throat is dry. "And then what happens to me?"

"I will put you down, as I've done with those who came before you."

"Do you hear yourself? You're talking about taking a life like it means nothing. Like I mean nothing!"

"Everyone on this earth has their place. Yours is to be the prey for me and my cousins."

My eyes water, but before I can respond, the Brute jumps to his feet, ripping off his mask. Everything feels like it slows around me. Henri stares back, pleading at me with his eyes. For what, I'm not sure. Forgiveness maybe?

"Henri?"

"I'm so sorry, Dove." His voice is broken, as if he really believes what he's saying.

"You're a part of this? Why?"

And how could he do this to me?

He shakes his head. "We don't have time. Dove, sweetheart, you have to believe me. I'm going to get you first. When I do, this will all be over, and we can go home."

I shouldn't trust him, but I do.

Beast snorts. "How very touching. Still making promises you can't keep, I see."

Henri glares. "Fuck off, Luca."

The Beast rips off his mask. There, before me, stands Luca Di Bello. The most feared man in Chicago. I feel like I'm going to be sick.

"Luca Di Bello is your cousin?" Something Henri said earlier crosses my mind. "The guns. You said your grandfather used to hunt game. Is this what you meant? Animals *and* people?"

The nod is barely detectable. Oh, my good god. These men have been trained their entire lives to hunt. I cannot outrun or outsmart them, especially on their own turf. Hope deflates out of me like air leaving a balloon.

Luca smirks. "I see you're seeing the bigger picture. It's true that your salvation lies in whomever catches you. Not only do you have to be caught, but you have to be brought to the finish line."

"Meaning?"

"Meaning that one of us might catch you, but it's entirely possible that the other two may steal you."

I glance at the Brain, who still wears his mask. That's what's going to happen, then. Two of them are going to work together. I meet Henri's gaze. Will he be able to save me?

Henri says in a low tone, "Dove, you have to try to win. There's always a chance that you can outsmart us."

My eyes water as I nod. I mean, what choice do I have unless I refuse to take part?

Luca says, "Just so we're clear. If you decide not to play with us, then it will be so much worse for you when I catch you. Understand?"

I glare. "Yes, I understand. But I have a few stipulations. I want to see Chip and Belle. I don't know any of you. Not really. I need to know that they're safe. Second, I want shoes. There's no way I'm going to outrun the three of you barefoot. Three, I want a ten-minute head start."

"Ten minutes? I don't think so."

"Afraid a chubby girl is going to manage to outrun you?"

He smiles at me. "Fine. I will agree to the head start and I will allow you to see proof of your sibling's safety. As for the shoes, that's a hard limit."

"Deal."

He snaps his fingers, and the Brain scurries away. I purposely turn my attention from him to Henri.

"I'm guessing this is why you didn't answer my text."

He flinches. "Dove, I—"

"Was this the plan all along? To seduce me so I'd let down my guard."

"I know I haven't given you any right to believe me, but that's not the case. I didn't know that Luca had his eyes set on you until it was too late."

Luca huffs at that. I look away. As crazy as it is, I believe Henri. I just don't understand why he's going along with this madness.

As if sensing my thoughts, he says, "I didn't have a choice. The only thing I could do was to take part so that I can be the one who wins you."

Luca chooses that moment to speak. "About that. Don't get it in your head that you can simply let my cousin catch you without fighting. Your punishment will be much worse if that's what happens."

The thought hadn't even crossed my mind, mostly because I still can't believe this is happening to me. The Brain comes back, carrying a tablet that he hands to Luca. Luca swipes on the screen before turning it so I can see. A sob works its way up my throat. It's video footage, and the timestamp shows it is current. Chip is asleep in a bed covered by a blanket from his favorite movie. He's surrounded by toys and is smiling even in his sleep. The camera moves, zooming in on Belle, who's in a crib on the other side of the room. She's asleep and looks as healthy as can be.

The room they're in is massive. Even in the dark, I can tell that the carpet is lush. Toys litter the floor, and it makes something deep in my chest pull. That room is bigger than our entire apartment. It's something I'll never be able to give them on my own. They're safe, warm, and unharmed. That right there is more than I've been able to give them.

"You swear that they're going to be taken care of?"

Luca puts the tablet face down on the tabletop. "I give you my word."

"When will the chase happen?"

"Now."

I swallow. "I'm ready."

I'm anything but ready, but I'll be damned if I let them know. Besides, I'd rather face my fate now than to have time to let it fester in the back of my mind.

Luca says, "Excellent. Let's go outside, shall we?"

He's acting like this is going to be something pleasant when it's not. What is wrong with this man?

He leads the way, and Henri follows right behind. I was hoping he would come to my side, but maybe that's against some kind of rule or something. The Brain follows behind me.

I glance over my shoulder. "Scared to take off your mask?"

"No."

But he makes no move to remove it. Creep.

I'm led outside, and it hits me just how big this estate is. We're clearly not in Chicago, though we have to be close since the car ride wasn't terribly long when I was kidnapped. The yard is well kept, but once we get to the back of the house, I see what Luca meant. It looks like the lawn has never been mowed. Trees line the property, and in the distance, I see a red, blinking light.

"Is that where I have to go to win?"

I hope like hell that they can't hear the doubt in my voice.

Luca answers, "Yes."

Even if I was in shape, I'm not sure that I'd be able to do this with ease. I glance at Luca, who's watching me with a smile on his lips. An actual smile.

He says, "Your time starts soon. After ten minutes, my cousins and I will give chase. After twenty, the hounds will be released."

"Excuse me. What?"

"Oh, did I forget to mention the dogs?" He gives me a look that sends my stomach swirling. "There are dogs. Six of them. All very good at what they do, in case you manage to outrun us and hide."

Brain adds, "Others have asked for a map of the property so they could figure out the best route." He clicks his tongue. "You might not be the smartest birdie we've ever had, but you're the prettiest."

My stomach heaves. I could have asked for a map, and they would have given it to me? The look on Henri's face confirms this. Shit. Shit! Shit! Shit!

Luca says, "Your time starts in one minute. I'd tell you to stretch or something, but I doubt it will make a difference. You've already put yourself at a disadvantage by refusing to eat. Remember that when I catch you. Remember that this could have been avoided so many times. Remember that I'm a man of my word. I will catch you. I will break you. And then I'm going to kill you."

Air solidifies in my throat. Each word that he says feels like a punch to the gut.

He smiles. "Better run, Dove."

I want to slap the look right off Luca's face. He thinks he's won this, and it pisses me off.

"Run."

# 10

### Dove

*"Run."*

Everything in my body screams for me to do as he says, but I know that as soon as I take off that my life is over. My best bet it is to stay right where I'm at. But what if he wasn't lying about the dogs? They'll attack me and I won't be able to get out of this hell.

Henri steps forward. "Dammit, Dove. Run!"

The anguished look in his eyes has me running. I'm still so angry and hurt by what Henri has done, but I have faith that he's going to catch me as he promised and get me out of this.

The ground is uneven, cutting into the soles of my feet. It could be worse—there could be snow on the ground. The weather gods must have a sense of humor because icy rain pours down at that moment, thunder rumbling in the distance. The red light seems so far away, but I can do this. I have to!

My lungs burn as I try to suck in oxygen. I've never been

a good runner, but this dress is slowing me down. I grab the skirt, lifting it without slowing my pace. Has it been ten minutes yet? I have no way of knowing. If I had been smart, I would have asked that they announced the time by firing a gun. *Should've, could've, would've*, I think bitterly. A rock cuts into the bottom of my foot, nearly tripping me. Hot tears sting the back of my eyes. How did I end up here? Luca said he's been watching me for months and I had no idea. What is it about me that would attract someone like him?

Ahead, I spot a stream. Maybe I can follow it, crossing back and forth to make it hard to track me. I jump into the water and regret it right away. It's so cold that it takes my breath away. Not only that, but it's super deep. I end up submerged and have to kick my way to the surface. The maxi dress clings to me until I feel claustrophobic. It also tries to pull me under, making fear course through me. By the time I get out of the water, I'm shivering and depleted of the precious energy that I have left in my body.

A gun shot rings in the air, and it's too close to comfort. Looks like I am going to get a warning, even though I didn't think to ask for one. Tears do fall from my eyes this time as I try to find the red light in the distance to reorientate myself. I finally spot it and realize that my little swim in the creek turned me all around. After slipping and sliding on the muddy bank of the creek, I finally reach solid ground. My teeth chatter as I stumble ahead. Each step sends a shooting pain up my leg into my back, and I'm not sure if it's because I'm so cold or if I hurt myself in the water.

Masculine laughter carries on the wind, but I don't stop to look and see if someone is close. It won't do any good. They know the layout of the land, so my best bet is to just keep moving. Only, it gets harder and harder with each step. My body is fighting against me to shut down. Luca's words cross my mind. He's right—this is my fault. I refused to eat, and now I'm weaker than I was before. A frustrated cry leaves my lips as I grab onto a tree to catch my breath.

Stopping is a mistake. I hear everything around me, and I know things aren't looking good for me. Footsteps pound against the earth, sounding closer than further away. I look up at the tree. It's too tall to climb. Even if I somehow managed to get up to a branch, my scent is all over the place. Once the dogs are released, they'll find me instantly. I hit the trunk of the tree. How am I going to get out of this? I'm so tired and I don't think I can bring myself to run.

A tree branch breaks, and it's close. So, what do I do? I run.

*Luca*

I creep closer to Dove. My entire body courses with energy only found during the hunt. My senses are tuned to what I seek, which is a scared woman who is doing nothing to protect herself. Her footsteps have been loud as she ran, but not as loud as her uncontrolled breathing. Her scent lingers in the air. When I let her shower, she thought I was being nice. The thought is laughable. No, she used the rose scented body wash without thought, and not her scent is everywhere. It makes my mouth water. It makes my cock hard. Fuck. The things I'm going to do to her once she's mine…

Dove whimpers as she tries in vain to hide. She's too

busy looking in the direction of where Henri is coming from to even notice that I'm there. I could grab her, but she's not broken enough. Not yet. I want her sobbing as she looks up at me, knowing that her life now belongs to me. Soon. But not soon enough.

Dove runs, as if that will save her, and Henri chases. Grandfather always said that Henri was too emotional in the chase. He'd let his feelings reign, which is why he never won. Not against me. Now is no exception. He chases Dove, gaining on her. She's the only thing in his sight. If he were wise, he'd look around to make sure I wasn't near, but he's always had more muscles than brains. I watch as Henri grabs Dove, pulling her to the ground. She screams, fighting him until she realizes who has her pinned. There's a tangible moment where they look at each other right before his mouth crashes over hers.

*Well, this is interesting.*

They kiss as if they feared they would never see each other again. And it fucking pisses me off. How dare he go after what's mine? Dove tenderly cups his face, whispering something. I can't make out the words from here, but it's enough that my cousin looks like he's been pierced right through the heart. They kiss again as they struggle to get as close as possible. Henri fumbles with his belt, unbuckling it and pulling down his pants just enough to free his cock. He moves between Dove's legs, showing her wet dress up around her waist and enters her in a thrust so powerful that her back pushes into the dirt. Her expression is marred in pain, but he kisses her until she rocks into his thrusts, her pain slowly replaced by pleasure. While he might be a brute, at least he has a heart. I won't be as gentle with her when I have her. And I *will* have her.

Henri's thrusts become shallow, and he reaches between

their joined bodies. Dove's mouth parts as a silent scream leaves her lips. Henri is close behind her, his release much louder. The look that passes between them pisses me off. One might say it looks like love. *Love.* The mere thought is laughable. Something pulls deep inside of my chest, and I turn my back on them. Reaching into my pocket, I send Maurice a text. Time to put my plan into action so that this game can be over, and I can take my prize back to the house.

Maurice texts back, and I smile at my phone. The prize is almost mine. Now I just need the Brute to fall for my trap. In the distance, the hounds howl as they're released from their cages. They, too, are excited about the chase. It's been too long since I've taken them out, letting them do what they do best. Dove and Henri stand, fixing their clothes. Dove's eyes are wide with fear, which makes me happy. Am I a beast for feeding off her fear? Yes. Do I care? Not in the least.

Henri says something, pointing in the opposite direction of the red light. Ah. He thinks he can save her by hiding her? He forgets that I know this land better than he does. But I'll let him do this. When the chase is over, I want both of them to know that Henri played a part in Dove being caught. Henri rips the hem of Dove's dress, so he can scent the area, and tells her to run. She takes off, like a scared little bird.

When Henri is alone, I step from the shadows.

"I wondered when you'd show your face." He doesn't even bother to look at me.

Pulling the gun from my waistband, I say, "And I wondered if you'd ever learn your lesson."

He turns to face me, his eyes widening. "Weapons weren't part of the deal."

"Neither were you."

I pull the trigger, watching as Henri falls to the ground. I move to stand over him. His eyes are glazed as he looks up at me.

"Don't worry. You won't die. But by the time you're able to move, it will be too late." I tap the barrel of the gun against his shoulder. "Horse tranquilizer. A bit ironic, don't you agree?"

He grunts as if he's trying to move, but he's only fighting a losing battle.

"I'm off to claim my prize. Once you're able to move, you'll be escorted from the property. I expect the ring by the end of the week, or there will be hell to pay."

Fire flashes in his eyes, and I laugh.

"Oh, it won't be you I hurt. Grandfather's will prevents that. It will be Dove who receives the punishment. Remember that when you think of going against me." I lean in, lowering my tone. "I have grand plans for her. Plans that would make you sick to your stomach. This isn't going to be a simple end for her. No, she's going to suffer longer than anyone else just because I know she means something to you."

I pat his cheek and stand. It's finally time to get my prize.

# 11

*Dove*

My legs tremble as I run. Henri said I'd be safe coming this way, and that he would find me as soon as he could. There's a voice deep inside of me that knows that this was a mistake. I was safer with him, but he told me to go, and so I did. But he should have caught up to me by now. He said it would only take a moment to put my scent in the wrong direction. My breath hitches in my throat. What if something happened to him? What will I do then?

Dogs howl in the distance, and this time I fall when I stumble. Pain shoots through my wrist as I scamper to my feet. Cradling my arm to my chest, I run, though each step brings pain so strong that black dots dance across my vision. Henri said there was an old hunting shack ahead, and that we could wait there until Luca had circled back to look for me. Ahead, I see the shack. It's barely standing, but I think he was right when he said it will be enough to hide us.

Using the last of my energy, I enter the shack and lean against the wall, where I'm out of sight. My wrist is hurting so badly that I don't want to risk looking at it in case I see something bad, like a protruding bone, so I close my eyes. It's risky allowing myself to get lost in my thoughts, but what else can I do until Henri gets back to me? I think about the way he tenderly kissed me after catching me. My cheeks warm at the thought of what came next. I can't believe we had sex. It's not how I imagined my first time, but I'm not mad about it. It was like... it was like we *had* to be with each other at that moment. Nothing else mattered.

I'm smiling when footsteps approach.

"I was worried you would not make it."

Luca Di Bello steps into the shack, and the smile leaves my face.

"Not who you expected?" His lips twitch. "I should have warned you that Henri has a tendency of letting people down. Just ask the Brain."

"Where is he?"

"Hmm. Right about now he's being taken back to his house to sleep off the tranquillizer I gave him." He clicks his tongue. "Poor Henri went down like a horse."

My stomach heaves, but I don't have time to process the news as Luca stalks toward me.

"Time to give up, little bird. Fighting me at this point will only make things worse."

I shake my head. "No. This isn't over yet."

"Have it your way. The Brain will be here with the hounds soon. I'm sure they'd love to give chase. I've been neglectful of them recently, so they would see this as a reward."

"You're sick."

"And you're mine. Do the smart thing, Dove. Come with me and we can end this now." His gaze goes to my wrist that I'm still cradling. "The terrain only gets worse from here.

You might have made it with Henri at your side, but that ship has sailed."

Defeat courses through me, though I try to fight it. There has to be a way to beat him. Dogs bark, and the sound is so close that I hear them panting, too. No! Luca stares at me, waiting for me to make my choice.

With a nod, I say, "I'll go with you."

"Wise choice, Dove. Come."

He leads me out of the cabin. I expect to see the Brain, but no one is there. Luca laughs at the look on my face.

"One thing you should know about me is that I will do anything to win." He gestures to a nearby tree. "There's a speaker mounted at the base. That's where the sound of the dogs was coming from."

"They were never out here?"

He shrugs. "Not yet. As I said, I've been neglectful. If I had let them out, there's a good chance they would have hurt you."

"As if you care."

"Oh, I do care, little bird. I'm the only one who gets to hurt you."

The seriousness with which he says those words has me stopping in my tracks.

"Don't even think about running. You'll only piss me off."

Over his shoulder, I see the red blinking light. We're closer to it than I thought. If I make it, then that means I win. His rules be damned. Pretending to be meek, I walk toward him. When I'm at his side, I shove him and then run as fast as I can. He curses once, but it's his laugher that propels me to run faster. Somehow, I manage to navigate over the terrain. The need to live overrules the pain that I feel. Instead, I push myself harder than I thought possible. And it works!

The light is close enough that I see it hangs atop a wooden pole. There's a rope hanging from it. That must be what I have to pull to show that I've arrived at the pole first. My sides burn and I know I'm running out of energy. If I don't do this, then I'm dead. Chip and Belle will grow up under the thumb of the Di Bello Family. While they'll be safe from my father, that doesn't mean they'll be safe from Luca. What if he makes them do the same thing I'm doing? I should have asked more questions and demanded that they be raised away from the Di Bello Family. A frustrated cry leaves my lips.

I'm so close that I see the Brain standing next to the pole. He pulls his mask off, his face showing his surprise that I'm about to beat Luca. Victory courses through me. I'm going to do this! I'm going to win! The Brain's mouth moves, but I can't hear what he's saying until it's too late.

"Look out!"

The words register at the same time something slams into me from the side. I scream as I hit the ground. Rock cut into my skin and I try in vain to cradle my already injured wrist. I'm rolled onto my stomach and something heavy mounts on my back. Hot breath hits the shell of my ear right before teeth scrape down, nipping my earlobe.

"I told you I always win, little bird."

I thrash, trying to get him off me. It doesn't work. He shifts, moving lower. And, god help me, I get wet between the legs as he presses my pubic bone into the dirt. It's not just that, though. All my senses feel like they're in overdrive. I hear the Brain laughing nearby. Rain falls on us. But what I really notice is the scent of sweat and leather that teases my nose. Luca shifts again, and his cock presses into my bottom. A soft moan works its way past my lips as he grabs my arms, pulling them behind my back. Belatedly, I realize he's cuffing my wrists together. Hot tears fill my eyes as he moves off me.

"Up."

He helps me to my feet, and I refuse to meet his gaze. Instead, I take the time to look over the Brain. There's a resemblance between him and Henri, except he's bald. He stares at me with sympathy, as if he knows the hell that I'm about to go through.

Luca says, "You did well, little bird."

Not well enough. This time I do look at him.

"What happens now?"

"We go back to the house where I will claim my prize."

"Wh-what does that mean?"

He smiles. "It means, my pet, that I'm going to fuck you, and I won't promise I'll be as gentle as the Brute was."

My eyes water at the mention of Henri.

"Before we go, I want to negotiate something."

"I don't believe you understand how negotiating works."

Ignoring him, I say, "I want Chip and Belle raised away from you and your family. I don't want them to end up like you, nor do I want you to decide you want to hunt them."

He nods. "Done."

Without saying another word, he drags me toward the pole, pulling the rope. The light switches from red to black. And just like that, I've lost. He tugs me to a waiting SUV. Getting in hurts, but I don't let him see. Instead, I stare out the window as he climbs in next to me. My heart is racing, and I feel like I'm going to be sick. He said he's going to fuck me. I shudder. How did I end up here? And what kind of monster thinks that this is okay?

The Brain gets in the driver's seat and starts the SUV.

Luca says, "Drive quickly, Maurice. My cock is aching to be inside of her."

The Brain, or Maurice, I guess, looks at us in the mirror. "Little birds, little birds. Oh, how pretty they sing when speared by the hunter."

He laughs at his own pun. All while I fight barfing all over the leather seats. It's a losing battle, though, and I gag right before vomiting on the floor. Luca makes a sound of disgust, uses a silk handkerchief to wipe my mouth since my hands are bound. By the time we reach the house, I think I'm going to be sick again. Luca hops out of the SUV, rounding to my side where he helps me out. He steps aside as I vomit again. This time it's more bile, which makes my throat burn.

"Finished?"

I glare, and he laughs. Gripping my arm, he pulls me behind him as we enter the house. There's a man that I've never seen before waiting with a medical bag.

Luca says, "I'm going to take off the cuffs. Try nothing stupid, or you'll regret it."

I nod my understanding. The cuffs come off, and I rub my injured wrist.

The man says, "May I look at it?"

Holding out my hand, he presses on it, and I wince.

"I think it's just a sprain. I won't know for sure unless I do an x-ray."

He glances at Luca, who shakes his head.

"Just leave materials so I can wrap it later."

The man does as he's told and bows toward Luca before leaving us.

"Why didn't you want him to x-ray it?"

"Because it doesn't matter if it's broken or not. You won't live long enough to see the bone heal."

My lips part, but no words come out.

He smiles. "Come. Let's get you cleaned up."

I follow him from the room, up the stairs. This time, we go to the west wing, opposite of where I was kept before. There aren't as many doors down this hallway, and it feels... colder. Emptier. And even a bit scarier.

Luca opens the last door, stepping aside for me to enter. My gaze goes to the golden cage in the center of the room. It looks like a cage for a bird, only it's the perfect size for a human. There's a swing that hangs by two chains, but other than that, it's empty. Luca closes the door behind me, and I hear a lock sliding into place.

He stands next to me. "It's beautiful, isn't it? Had it made just for you."

"You're sick."

He shrugs. "I've been called worse. Come."

We walk around the cage, past his massive bed, to a door that leads to the biggest bathroom I've ever seen in my life. If I wasn't scared that my life was about to end, I'd take the time to appreciate how luxurious the room was. Instead, I watch as he goes to the massive walk-in shower and turns on the water. Steam fills the room, and he turns to me.

"Get naked."

If there was anything left in my stomach, I'm sure I'd be vomiting right now. He stares at me with a hardened glare that has me moving. I will never admit it, but it's a relief to get the icy cold material away from my skin. But standing naked before him presents a whole new set of problems, especially when his gaze trails slowly down my body. To make matters worse, my body reacts. My nipples harden and there's a rush of moisture between my legs.

"In."

I scurry inside just to get away from him. What I don't expect is for him to remove his clothes and join me.

"Wh-what are you doing?"

"Showering."

He reaches past me and grabs the shampoo. As he pours it into his hand, the same rose scent from my shower earlier fills the air.

"Didn't peg you as a floral guy."

"This isn't for me. It's for you."

I'm shocked as hell as he rubs the shampoo into my dark locks, lathering it.

"You bought me shampoo?"

"No." My chest falls as he continues, "All the women who take part in the hunt use the same products in case we have to send out the hounds. They're trained to find this scent."

Now I feel like the world's biggest idiot. When I was allowed to bathe earlier, it never crossed my mind that I would do something that would help my captors find me.

"I guess I made it pretty easy on you, didn't I?" I huff. "God, no wonder my father sold me."

"I would have had you even if your father hadn't agreed to the sale."

"Is that supposed to make me feel better?"

He's silent as he finishes washing my hair. The next bottle that he opens is more masculine scented, and he uses it for his own hair. Looking up, I can see how this shower was meant to be used for two people. There are two shower heads and jets, so that each person can enjoy themselves. Well, in most cases. Right now, this just feels like I'm walking slowly to my death with no way to stop.

Luca tips my chin. "Time to wash our bodies."

I reach for the loofah, but he stops me. Instead, he takes

it, adding body wash to it. My body is on fire as he washes me. When he gets to the junction between my legs, I try to stop him, but he only slaps at my hand.

"Little bird," he warns.

"This is embarrassing, okay? I don't like people touching me."

Or looking at me, really.

"You seemed to have no problem letting *Henri* touch you."

He says Henri's name with so much venom that I laugh.

"Are you jealous?"

He stands, towering over me. "No."

With that, the mood has shifted. He washes his own body and we both rinse off. He steps out of the shower, and I follow, reaching for a towel. My finger barely brushes it before he grabs me, tossing me over his shoulder. He marches from the bathroom to the bedroom, tossing me on his bed. My heart pounds and I scramble away from him, but it's no use. He moves over me, our wet bodies sliding against each other. But the thing I notice the most? His massive cock pressing against my stomach.

"I'm not fucking jealous of him or any other man. He did me a favor by fucking you first, so I don't have to be gentle."

"Please, don't do this."

He lowers so his nose touches the side of my face. I fight shivering at the close contact.

"Don't act like you don't want this, too, little bird. I felt the way your body responded to me when I caught you in the field. You *liked* it, just like you're going to like this."

"You're delusional."

He sighs. "Guess we're going to have to do this the hard way."

Grabbing my injured wrist, he pulls it toward the top of

the bedframe. I cry out, but he ignores me and the pain he's causing. Instead, he cuffs my wrist before doing the same to my other wrist. Next are my legs until I'm literally spread out before him. Standing, he goes to the nightstand next to the bed and comes back with a tube. Popping the cap, he smears a generous amount on his fingers and then rubs it between my legs. My hips lift as I try to get away from his intrusive fingers, but he doesn't stop until I feel a warming sensation. Holy mother of god. Grinning wickedly, he takes the tube of lube and swipes it against each of my nipples. In horror, I watch as my body betrays me, becoming aroused by the tingling sensation between my legs and on my nipples.

Luca says, "I think this will go much better now."

I want to tell him to fuck off, but all thoughts disappear when he blows on one of my nipples. It hardens, begging to be sucked. He doesn't suck it, though. Instead, he flicks it with his finger. My hips arch off the bed, which sends another rush of moisture between my legs. My eyes water. This is so fucked up!

Without breaking eye contact, he lowers his head and kisses the peaked skin. A deep moan works its way up my throat when his tongue flicks against the bud. At the same time, his other hand goes between my legs. Even if he hadn't used lube, I'd be wet by now. He finds my clit and rubs it until my eyes close and I rock into his touch.

"Eyes open. I want you to know who's making you feel this way."

Again, there's a jealous note to his voice. Is he worried that I'm thinking about Henri? The thought sends more heat rushing through my body. He covers my nipple with his mouth, licking and sucking until I'm making sounds. I couldn't stop even if I wanted to. The thing is... if I'm going to die tonight, then I want to enjoy this. So, I don't feel bad when I whisper his name, urging him on.

"That's right, little bird. I'm the one making you feel good."

He slips a finger inside of me and I moan.

"Yes, so good, Luca. I need more."

"Such a greedy little slut, aren't you? What do you need, little bird? Tell me."

"Your cock. I need you to fill me."

The words leave my lips in a rush, and I'm rewarded with a long suck on my nipple that has me whimpering as my orgasm rushes closer.

"Please," I beg. "Please fuck me!"

He moves over me, and I pant in anticipation as he rubs his cock through my folds before entering me. We both moan as he thrusts until he's deep inside of me. He's bigger than Henri, but not by much. My pussy is tender, but all thoughts fade as he moves again.

"Fuck, you're fucking perfect. I knew you would be, too. Your body was made for me. This pussy was made for me."

"Yes," I agree.

His hand goes around my neck, and he squeezes as he looks down at me. We both know that he could end me right now, and that seems to turn both of us on. My pussy flutters as I shatter around him. Little black spots dance around my vision, but he doesn't loosen his grip. Instead, he pounds into me while I struggle to breathe. Everything feels dull, but I can still feel him deep inside of me, as if he's saying he's not going to let me go until he says it's time.

My lips part as I use the last of my oxygen. He removes his hand and comes, filling me with his cum. I shatter, too, whether from pleasure or the joy of being alive, I'm not sure.

I'm still gasping for air as he pulls out of me. Holy hell, that was... intense.

He stands, his cock still hard. I'm not sure how that's even possible. Reaching over, he presses a button that releases the cuffs on my ankles and wrists.

"Time for you to get in the cage."

"What?"

"You heard me." He motions to the cage. "In."

I stand, surprised my legs can still hold me. Unsteadily, I cross the room to the cage. He follows, opening the door.

"Why do I have to go in there?"

"Because all pets must be kept in cages. Now, in you go."

A numbness settles over me.

"I thought you were going to kill me once you fucked me."

He smirks. "Now that I've had a taste, I think I'll wait. Use you some more. We both know you'll like it, too."

"I hate you."

"It doesn't matter what you feel."

He closes the door, locking it. I hate how carelessly he crosses the room to the bed that he just ravished me in and climbs under the covers. A moment later, the lights go off and I'm surrounded by darkness. Siting on the floor, every thought that I've tried to avoid crashes into me. Hot tears fill my eyes as my reality sets in.

I had sex with Luca Di Bello. Now only that, but I begged him to fuck me. Closing my eyes, I allow the truth to seep into my bones. This is my fault, no matter how much I want to blame him. And that's something that I have to live with.

# 12

*Dove*

When I awaken, I'm alone in the room. My body aches, and it can't all be blamed from sleeping on the hard floor of the cage. No, I ache because of Luca and all the things he did to me. The most terrible part is that I liked what happened as much as when Henri took me in the field. Groaning, I cover my face with my hands. What is wrong with me?

The door opens and Maurice enters carrying a food tray. He sets it on the table that slide inside the cage and then crosses the room to the curtains, opening them. Sunlight fills the room but doesn't seem to quite reach me. There's symbolism in that, I'm sure.

"Morning, little birdie. Did you sleep well in your cage?"

He asks so cheerfully that I laugh.

"Are you joking?"

"Why would I joke?"

"Because I'm being kept in a freaking cage against my will and I'm buck-naked. No, I didn't sleep well!"

He turns to face me. "But the cage is inside. Things

could be much worse for you. As for clothes, I can get something for you to wear."

He leaves, coming back with a robe that he slides through the bars. I take it, putting it on. It's not much, but it's better than nothing.

"Thanks."

He nods, going back to the window.

"You're Maurice? Why do they call you the Brain?"

"The same reason they call Luca the Beast and Ri the Brute."

Ri? He must mean Henri. Does the nickname mean they're closer than he and Luca are?

"So you're smart then?"

"That depends on who you ask."

"I suppose if I had a nickname, it would be an idiot. Maybe dense. Slut. Fat." I sigh. "The choices are endless, really."

"You would be none of those things. You'd be the Bird. The piece that completes us." His face falls. "But Luca will never let us keep you. He doesn't like to share."

I get the feeling that he's not exaggerating.

"How many others have there been? Before me..."

He thinks. "At least ten, though that's debatable because Grandfather would want us to count the ones we practiced on. He wanted to make sure we knew our roles."

"Does Luca always win?"

"Not always." A ghost of a smile lifts his lips upward. "I beat him once. Ri has beat him three times."

So he doesn't always win. That's good to know.

"But Luca has made certain accommodations that ensure he wins each time now. He knows the land better than anyone, and he knows where the booby traps are."

"Booby traps?"

"Oh, yes. It's amazing that you didn't step on any, though Ri must have an idea that they're out there since he steered you away from them."

"What kind of booby traps?"

"Bear traps. Holes that are so deep you'd never be able to get out on your own."

"And the dogs?"

He frowns. "I hate that he uses the hounds to hunt people. They only want to hunt birds. *Real* birds. But Luca won't let them. It makes me sad."

"Then maybe you should think about who you work for."

"I don't work for Luca. I work *with* him. It's the way it's always been in our family." He sighs. "Birdies chirping hurt my head. I'm going to leave."

He walks away, closing the door behind him. The whole interaction with him was... strange. He's called the Brain, which means he must be smart, but maybe it's more like a play on words. He speaks in riddles, making it hard to understand what he means.

"What happened to you, you poor man?" I whisper to the empty room.

Sighing, I go to the food tray. I made the mistake once of not eating. I won't do it again.

The rest of the day goes by slowly. No one comes to check on me. I really need to pee, but there's nowhere to go. Moving around the cage for the thousand time I come to a stop at a hole in the floor. This better not be what I freaking think it is. The door opens, and Luca enters. I exhale. Thank god.

"I need to use the restroom."

He eyes me. "There's a hole in the bottom of the cage for you to use."

"Are you out of your mind?"

He goes to the minibar, pouring himself a drink. "Some might say I am. Don't worry, little bird. I won't watch while you relieve yourself."

He smiles as he leaves. Jerk! Glancing at the hole, I bite back a groan. *I really need to go...*

So, I do what needs to be done. Thank god Maurice gave me a robe to wear. This way, I'm not exposed to anyone who might be watching. Looking around the room, I spot at least two cameras. Yeah, Luca is probably watching somewhere. Finishing, I stand. My stomach rumbles, making me wish I had saved the bread from my morning tray. If I get fed again, I will save some.

Time creeps by again. This time, I watch as the sun lowers into the sky until the stars come out. There are low clouds making me think it might rain again tonight. Maybe even snow. Chip loves the snow. My eyes water. Is he okay? Is he missing me?

There are tears streaming down my face when Luca enters the room again. He goes to the bathroom, and a moment later, I hear running water. When he walks out nude, my mouth waters and I hate myself for it.

"Take off the robe."

"What?"

He goes to the door of the cage, unlocking it.

"Take off the robe, Dove. Don't make me say it again."

My hands tremble as I do what he says. He leads me to the bed, motioning for me to climb on it.

"So that's how it is? You ignored me all day and now you want to have sex?"

"Smart girl. Spread your legs."

Glaring at him, I do as he says. I want to say that I fought him. I want to say that I didn't enjoy it as he made me come more times than I could count. But I can't.

Days bleed into weeks and maybe even months as the same routine continues. I wake up each morning alone. Maurice brings me breakfast. Sometimes I'm allowed to shower. Most often I'm not. The curtains are always open during the daytime so I can see out. I watch as the leaves on the trees fall. I watch as snow covers the ground. Life moves on without me. I hate it. I constantly wonder how Chip and Belle are doing. Do they even ask about me? Do they think that I left them? All things I'll never get answers to since Luca refuses to talk about them.

At the end of each day, Luca returns and opens the door of the cage. He takes me to the bed and uses me until we're both spent. He doesn't even have to use the cuffs on me. No, I go willingly just to get out of the cage, or so I tell myself.

One night, he surprises me by pulling me close to his body after making me come at least four times.

"What were you going to school for?"

I look over to make sure he's not on the phone, talking to someone else. He's not.

"I was mostly just trying to get my basics out of the way."

"I'm sure you had goals or dreams, though."

I shift, making myself comfortable. "Maybe. I tried not to think too far ahead, you know? I was looking at something in healthcare since there's always work there, or so people say."

"What would you do if you could do anything in the world?"

I smile. "When I was little, I used to tell my dad that I

wanted to be a mom. Probably because I never had one. I think working with underprivileged kids would be something close to that. Helping kids who are growing up in the same way I did."

He grunts and doesn't answer.

"What about you?"

"Me?"

"What would you be doing if this life hadn't been thrust upon you?" At his curious look, I say, "Maurice said that you were each raised from young boys to live this life."

He rubs his chest, right over his heart. "I've never thought about it, I guess."

We're both silent, lost in our own thoughts. Just as I'm getting sleepy, he moves away from me.

"Time to get back in your cage, little bird."

And just like that, I'm back to hating Luca Di Bello.

The next morning he's gone, and my feelings are still hurt. Freaking jerk! Does he get off on being nice to me only to turn around and be mean? He must! Maurice enters right on time.

"Good morning, birdie."

I don't answer and turn my back on him.

"Luca said you were mad. I guess he was right."

That only gets a huff out of me. He places the food tray on the table, sliding it toward me. I make no moves to get it, and he rounds the cage so he can see me.

"Are you okay, birdie?"

"My name is Dove, and, no, I'm not okay."

He stares at me before nodding. "Then I will stay and keep you company. I just need to grab something."

He leaves and I hope he doesn't return. Sadly, he does. This time he carries a toolbox and an old gun. He goes to the table by the window, spreading out his items. The sunlight reflects off his bald head. I wonder if he ever gets sunburned there. His skin tone is fair, as if he doesn't get out much. My gaze goes past him, to the window. I'd give anything to go outside and sit in the sun. Even if it's the middle of winter.

Maurice hums to himself as it works, and it's oddly comforting. I'll never admit it, though. He takes apart the gun, cleaning it until it shines. Then he puts it back together. I'm about to comment that he's done this before when he takes the gun apart again. He repeats the process over and over, never looking my way. Is he like this because of his grandfather? Luca even?

"Why do you keep rebuilding it?"

"I like it when things feel right," he answers, as if it's the most obvious thing in the world.

"How does it feel right?"

"Taking it apart is easy. Anyone can do that. Putting it together takes skill. Part of that skill is knowing when the parts are in the right place. Everything clicks, like you and I are clicking right now."

That makes me smile.

"If I didn't know any better, I'd say you were flirting with me."

I'm teasing, but he stills.

"No, that's not what this is. You need a friend and I need a friend. That's it." He drops the pieces in his hand and tosses them into his toolbox. "The Beast would hurt me if he thought I liked you like *that*."

"Maurice, it's okay. I was only teasing. I know you don't like me like *that*."

I echo his words to ease his mind, but it doesn't seem to

work. He appears more agitated than before. Wait. Does he have a crush on me? His cheeks are a light shade of pink and he won't look me in the eyes. Oh my goodness.

"Maurice..."

"It doesn't matter how I feel, birdie. You're not mine and soon Luca will tire of you." He stands. "I'll be back."

I feel terrible and call after him, but he ignores me. I truly had no idea that he had a crush on me. I mean, he's easy on the eyes. I wonder why he doesn't think that I could like him back? And would Luca really be angry if he knew that Maurice had a crush on me? Probably so. Freaking jerk!

I'm deep in thought when Maurice returns. He's silent as he goes to the window, staring out.

"You don't have to stay if you don't want to." I pause. "And, for what it's worth, I'm sorry."

"Sorry?"

"For upsetting you."

He doesn't answer, but turns to look at me. He's done this before, and I just assumed it was to report back to Luca. Maybe there's more to it than that. I stare back, unblinking. He's as tall as Henri and Luca and still favors Henri. His eyes are blue, and one has a swirl of green around the pupil. His head is bald, and it looks to be a natural thing versus shaving. He's leaner than both Henri and Luca, but I bet he could give them a run for their money in a fight since he's so smart. There's a scar above his upper lip that's barely noticeable. I wonder what happened to him. I don't want to ask, though, because we've settled into a peaceful silence.

Needing to move, I climb onto the swing. There's not much to do in the cage, but being on the swing gives me the opportunity to look outside to the yard. The grass is covered in a light dusting of snow, meaning we're in November.

Possibly even December. My breath hitches. Chip always loves this time of the year.

"Don't cry, birdie. Swing. It will make your heart lighter."

I don't answer, but do as he suggests. He watches me. It's still unnerving the way he stares without blinking, as if he's getting lost in his head. The metal bar cuts into my bottom, so I shift, trying to get comfortable.

Maurice says, "Moving only makes it hurt more."

"Thanks, captain obvious. If you're such an expert on being held in a cage, then please enlighten me on how to make this more enjoyable."

He snorts and moves closer.

"You're not supposed to enjoy it. This is all for Luca's pleasure. He's a lot like our grandfather. At least you can move in yours. The one I was in was so small that I could only lie curled in a ball. Grandfather thought it would help with the claustrophobia." He touches the bar of the cage. "He was wrong."

"How old were you?"

"Six."

My mind immediately goes to Chip. How could someone do that to an innocent child?

Maurice meets my gaze. "It wasn't the last time he caged me, but it's what I remember the most. It's when I learned that going inside of my head was the safest place to be."

"And how does one do that?"

"Practice."

He walks away, but I call out to him. "Please don't go. I... I don't think I can stand being alone and I'm not sure when or if Henri is coming back."

"Ri will be back as soon as he can." He smiles. "He's never let me down. Not once."

"It sounds like you're closer to him than to Luca. Why do you work with Luca, then?"

"No one wants to make the Beast mad. And I have enough brains to know that."

He walks away, leaving me to my thoughts. The crazy thing is, I really do wish he'd come back. I want to know more about the Brain. And that is quite surprising, indeed.

# 13

*Luca*

I'm distracted. I never get fucking distracted. My mind keeps going back to Dove, and the way I tried to get her to open up last night. Me. I was trying to make small talk with a woman in my fucking bed like we were in a relationship or something. Cursing, I close my laptop and turn to the window, looking out. I should have killed her the first night after I had her.

My phone rings and I glance at the screen. It's Mrs. Lansbury, the woman I hired to look after Dove's siblings. She's called daily with updates, truly thinking that I had taken them under my wings out of the goodness of my heart. I let the call go to voicemail. She's likely wanting to know when I'm going to move them from the city to one of my estates in another state. The old woman does not know that the request came from Dove, of course. She thinks that I want the kids to grow up where they can run and be outside as much as they want.

My phone vibrates as a voicemail comes through. She'll

likely tell me what they had to eat and say what good kids they are. I know she'll also say how much Chip misses Dove. She thinks Dove is dead and I haven't corrected her. It's better if the boy believes it, too. He's young enough that the pain will fade with time. I should know.

Cursing under my breath, I grab my phone and keys. I don't want to be here, trapped in my office. Making my way out of my office to the VIP area, I'm surprised to see Hook and his wife, Amelia, at the table reserved for Hook and CO. Hook glares when he sees me, but Amelia smiles. And, somehow, I find myself stopping.

"To what do I owe the pleasure?"

Hook scoffs before answering, "Just taking my lovely wife out on a date."

Amelia adds, "It's our anniversary."

I didn't think they had been together long enough to have an anniversary, but she did just have twins, so what do I know?

Hook says, "I've been meaning to ask you about something. I heard you were looking for David Potts a few months ago. He washed up near Navy Pier today, or what was left of him."

I bite back a smile. "Pity. Guess I won't get my money from him after all."

"Yes, pity." He takes a drink before asking, "Should I be expecting more bodies to wash up? I hear his eldest daughter is missing. And the rumor out of Neverland is that you recently hired a nanny."

"I do not know what you're talking about. As for the bodies, I'll let you know. Never can tell in our line of work, after all."

He curses, and his wife touches his arm as I walk away. I can't stand that fucker. He's always thought he was better than me because he was Midas' favorite. Well, fuck all of them. I don't need their approval.

My SUV is waiting when I get outside. What I don't expect is to find Henri sitting in the back seat when I climb in.

"Fucking hell. Who in the fuck let you in?"

"Your driver had enough sense to let me in. The alternative was him ending up in pieces at the bottom of the lake."

I snort. Guess I spoke too soon to Hook.

"You think this is funny?"

"Not in the least. Not only am I about to kick you out, but now I have to find a new driver. We both know how hard they are to come by."

Pierre has the nerve to flinch from the driver's seat.

"I'm not getting out until I know." His throat bobs. "Is she alive?"

"She is."

"Thank god."

"She's still going to die, Brute. Don't mistake what I'm saying. You still haven't produced the ring, and I need her as leverage."

He reaches into his pocket, handing me a box I'd know anywhere. I've thought about this moment since I was a young boy. I just knew there would be a sense of peace that came with finally having the ring. I didn't expect to feel nothing. In fact, it's kind of anticlimactic.

"There. Now do something good for once in your life and let her go."

"No can do. You've been balls deep inside of that pussy. You know how good it is."

"You bastard."

I laugh. "You're as much of a bastard as me, in case you've forgotten. Now get the fuck out of my vehicle before I forget the clause that says I can't blow your head off."

He stares at me before opening the door. "Don't think this is over."

"It was over the moment I laid eyes on her."

Tapping the roof, Pierre finally does what he's fucking supposed to and drives. Reaching for the box, I open it. I never doubted that the ring would be in here. Even Henri isn't that stupid. The ring sits on a velvet pillow that's faded. It's strange—when I was a kid, I'd look in this box and think how fancy it was. How Grandfather must have spent a ton of money when he bought it for his first wife.

I know the truth now. He didn't buy the ring; he stole it on the same night he stole our grandmother. He forced her to wear the ring, a sign that she was his property. After she gave him his first heir, he made her take part in the hunt and killed her in the end. His second and third wives met similar fates, though I've heard rumors he held onto the third wife longer than the rest. Her son was Maurice's father. I've often wondered if that's why he was so hard on Maurice growing up. Because he looks like his dad, which means he must resemble his grandmother a bit, too.

My father was the first son born into the family. He lived a life much like Grandfather and stole a bride, who also wore this ring. My mother. Only, he never got a chance to have her take part in the hunt. My grip tightens on the box. Grandfather suspected that my father was plotting against him, or so he claimed, and removed him from the picture after it was confirmed that a male heir was on the way. Me.

Mother spent the rest of her life in a cage very similar to the one Dove is in. Once I was born, she was taken out back. Grandfather never told me the specifics, but she never made it back into the house. Henri's father was now the next in line for the throne. Following in my father's footsteps, he picked a bride and gave her the ring. But he met the same fate as his brother as did Maurice's father. Their wives each died after giving birth. Maurice once told me he thinks his mother and father are together in the afterlife. I simply laughed at the notion.

We grew up under the firm hand of Grandfather, knowing what was expected of us one day. We were to find a bride, produce a male heir, and then enter our brides in the hunt. I'm not naïve—if Grandfather were still alive, there's a very good chance I'd already be dead. He'd say that I was planning to overturn him, and he would have been right.

Lifting the ring, the ruby rose sparkles in the light. Henri probably thinks that I plan to marry Dove, and that's why I wanted the ring. Marriage is the last thing that I want, and I have no desire to produce an heir. No, this ring means so much more. It means that I've finally beaten Grandfather at his own game. The hunt will stop with the three of us, and our fucked-up legacy will die when we do. As long as Henri and Maurice don't try to rally against me, then we'll all live long lives. Something none of us thought was possible.

So why does the thought of Dove wearing this ring make my dick throb?

Cursing, I place the ring in the box and snap it shut.

"Take me to Hôtel de Lumière."

I've been neglecting the hotel, and it's time to rectify that. The staff are surprised to see me, which makes me think they're hiding something. I bypass them, going to the manager's office. He's on the phone and pales when he sees me.

"I'll call you back." Dropping the phone on the cradle, he stands. "Mr. Di Bello. I wasn't expecting you."

"So I can see. Tell me, Stanley, what are you hiding?"

He pales even more. "Nothing. I swear."

"You know what the punishment is for lying to me," I warn him. "Sure you want to go with that answer?"

"I have done nothing except my job, Mr. Di Bello." He swipes at a piece of hair that's fallen across his forehead. "Guillaume D'Arque stopped by a few nights ago, but we made sure he left."

"D'Arque was here, and no one thought to call me?"

My fist clenches and I have to fight the urge not to punch Stanley. D'Arque may be the only man with big enough balls to openly challenge me. And he was here? Why?

"What did he say?"

"He said he heard you hadn't been at the bar or casino as much. He wanted to see if you were at the hotel. And I told him..."

"You told him *what*?" Venom laces my words.

"I told him we hadn't heard from you since the night that the young woman was removed from the hotel."

Mother fucking hell!

"I will deal with you later. If I were you, I'd start packing my desk."

And run. I don't mention this part, because I'm going to take deep satisfaction in killing this little rat. Going outside, I do something I never expected to have to do. I pull out my phone and call Henri.

"What?"

"We have a problem."

He snorts. "So now there's a 'we'? I don't think so, Luca."

"Guillaume D'Arque was at the hotel asking questions."

"What?"

"And my fucking hotel manager told him I hadn't been around since the night Dove was removed. He's a smart man and it won't be hard for him to piece things together."

I'm met with silence, which isn't exactly what I expected. Finally, Henri says, "I can meet you in ten minutes."

"The bar?"

"No, my place. I'm going to need weapons."

Ending the call, I tell Pierre where we're headed and then gaze out the window. D'Arque is going to find out the hard way what it means to fuck with me and my property.

---

Days bleed into each other as Henri and I work side by side, trying to flush out D'Arque. He's a crafty bastard and we miss him by an inch each day. If George Peters wasn't already dead, I'd suspect he was helping D'Arque hide. Henri and I are in one of our warehouses, cleaning up our latest kill, when my phone rings.

"You good?"

Henri grunts, and I walk to the other room before answering.

"Midas. To what do I owe the pleasure to."

"Cut the bullshit, Di Bello. What in the fuck is going on?"

"I do not know what you mean."

"I've been getting daily reports on the carnage you're creating. If they weren't all linked to Guillaume D'Arque, I'd be worried."

Midas knows of the beef between our families. He's also in agreement that the city will be better without him around.

"Just getting rid of a few bad seeds."

"Cut the bull. If you need help, just say so. Ronan is

chomping at the bit to kill someone. Huntsman feels the same. And you know the Behr brothers are always up for some house cleaning."

The chainsaw turns on in the other room and I move further away, hoping the sound doesn't carry.

"I'm fine."

"People who are fine don't have chainsaws running in the background."

"Heard that, did ya?"

"Luca." He sighs. "Let us help."

I snort. "And then owe all the Families a favor? I think not."

"Believe it or not, son, we would help you, expecting nothing in return. I know Alivse did a number on you boys, and you're leery of trusting others. Let me say it again. We're here if you need us."

Midas might be the only fucking person in this world with the balls to speak of Grandfather, but, then again, he ruled over Grandfather, so he earned that right. If Grandfather had his way, he would have killed Midas. But Midas was just that good.

I say, "I will keep it in mind. For now, I've got things under control."

Midas sighs, as if he's disappointed.

"We're here if you need us. Oh, and Hook has one request."

"Stop dumping the bodies in the lake. Kindly remind him it's the lake or the river. Either way, it's going to wash up on his shores."

Midas laughs. "Speak to you soon."

Ending the call, I tuck my phone in my pocket and join Henri in the other room. He's finished bagging up the body parts. All that's left is to wash down the concrete.

"Who was that?"

"Midas."

"He must be getting upset by the body count."

I grin. "Yeah. He said he and the other Families were there if we needed help, but I think we're doing just fine."

Henri points at me. "You're bleeding."

Looking down, I see where my black shirt is dark with blood. Shit. I'd felt a sting when we caught D'Arque's man, but didn't think about it once we got to the warehouse.

"Guess I should get home and clean this up."

Henri pauses, and I know something's on his mind. We've worked well together, all in the name of making sure Dove is protected. The irony isn't lost on me because I still plan to kill her.

He says, "I know this isn't what you want to hear, but I think you should let Dove go."

"Fucking hell, Henri."

"Hear me out. D'Arque knows about her, which means he sees her as a pawn that he can use against you. Keeping her makes you weak."

"And letting her go is the solution? Come on, Henri. We both know he'll get her as soon as I let her go."

"I'll keep her safe. You have my word."

"My answer is no."

He stares at me. "You know, one might suspect that you're getting feelings for her and that's why you don't want to let her go."

"Fuck off, Henri."

I walk away, ignoring him and the fact that I can't deny what he says.

# 14

*Dove*

There's something wrong with me. That's the only explanation for why I'm glad to see Luca. He strolls into the room, tossing his suit jacket on the chair by the fireplace. Going to the minibar, he pours a drink and tosses it back.

"Bad day?"

I shouldn't ask, because that might give him the impression that I'm curious or even that I care.

He huffs. "Only the usual bullshit."

"That sounds like a broad statement."

He pours another drink and crosses the room, staring up at me. Deep in thought, he rubs the rim of the glass against his bottom lip, and my traitorous body takes notice. It would be so much easier to hate him if I didn't find him attractive.

He says, "Chicago is split into three territories. We each handle our part of the city. Not only that, but we also have legal businesses that serve as fronts in case outsiders decide to look into us."

"Which part do you run?"

I've seen the Di Bello name around, but I guess I've never given it much thought to which part they might control.

"The Di Bello Family handles the north part of town, but, as I'm sure you've guessed, some businesses are in the south." He rubs his lip again before taking a drink. "One might think that the casinos or bars bring in the most money, but it's really Hôtel de Lumière that brings in the cash."

I nod. "I can see that."

He smirks. "You can? And why is that?"

"There's something about that hotel that makes you feel you're entering a different time in a different country. It's unlike all the other hotels in Chicago, and I think people can recognize that."

He hums but doesn't answer.

"So, what's the problem?"

"Business has been down at the hotel, and no one on my fucking team can figure out why."

I'm not sure if he even cares what my opinions are, but I say, "Well, the price might be one thing holding you back. Six hundred, and that's on a normal night. Just so we're clear, that's one-third of one of my paychecks. The average person can't justify spending that kind of money, but maybe they're not your target audience."

"Go on."

"Second, the man running the front desk is rude and scary. When I approached the front desk, he made it known that he didn't think I was good enough to grace the lobby of Hôtel de Lumière." I shake my head. "In retrospect, his reaction should have probably sent me packing."

"I would have still found you."

I loathe that his fucked-up words go right to my heart.

"I also think you could make it more inviting for families with kids. Right now, it feels like you only cater to rich men in the mafia who aren't traveling with their wives and kids."

He laughs at that. "You've got me there. Tell me, little bird. How have you managed to see what my team couldn't?"

"Are they men who work for you?"

"Yes."

"There's your answer. Try diversifying your team and see what you come up with."

"I just might do that." He finishes his drink. "Ready to come out for the night?"

My pulse skitters in my neck, but I nod. Reaching into his pocket, he pulls out the golden key that unlocks my cage. Stepping aside, he lets me walk by without grabbing for me.

"I'm going to shower."

He leaves me standing in the middle of his room, unsure of what to do with myself. I already know the door is locked, but I still try to open it. As I suspected, it doesn't open. The water turns on in the bathroom. An image of Luca in there, under the spray crosses my mind. What in the heck is wrong with me? He's the enemy! I shouldn't be sitting here thinking about how sexy he would look with water running over his chiseled body. I should look for a weapon or try any and everything to get out of here. I shouldn't cross the room and peer into the bathroom.

Luca stands next to the shower, rubbing his temples. He's nude, but what has me gasping are the bruises on his body.

"What happened?"

He turns, and I try like hell to ignore that he's hard.

"What are you doing in here, Dove?"

"You're bleeding!"

There's a cut on his side that looks bad.

He laughs. "It's nothing."

"Let me be the judge of that."

I expect him to tell me to leave. What I don't expect is for him to lean against the glass wall of the shower so I can examine his wound. The blood has mostly clotted, but the gash runs several inches.

"I don't think it's going to need stitches. How did it happen?"

He exhales through his nose as I run my finger over the length of the wound.

"Let's just say it happened on the not-so-legal side of the business."

"Did you win?"

"I always win."

Without thinking, I lean forward and press my lips against the wound. "Good."

"You're playing with fire, little bird. I hope you know that."

"Maybe I want to play with fire." I straighten, looking him in the eyes. "Maybe I want to get burned."

"And maybe we'll both burn together."

This is a bad idea, and yet I can't seem to stop. Without breaking eye contact, I untie the robe I'm wearing and let it drop to the ground. He eyes me as I stand before him, as naked as he is. Moving around him, I step into the shower under the spray of water. He watches as I get my hair wet and then reach for the shampoo. I'm doubting my plan. Maybe he doesn't feel the same for me? Tears fill my eyes and I turn under the spray of water to hide them.

"Are you hiding from me, little bird?"

He's close. I don't have to open my eyes to know that. Heat rolls off his body in waves, making me shiver.

"I wasn't sure if you were going to join me," I admit.

"I shouldn't."

It's all he says, but his fingers dig into my scalp as he lathers the shampoo. Closing my eyes, I tilt my head so he can wash my hair. We're both silent as we shower, likely lost in our own heads. I keep wishing that he'd kiss me. Touch me. Anything. He only touches me to wash me. And there certainly aren't any kisses, though I think I feel his lips brush against my shoulder as he turns off the water.

Feeling dejected, I move past him when he grabs my arm.

"I shouldn't do a lot of things where you are concerned, and yet here we are."

I search his gaze. "What other things do you want to do to me?"

"Terrible things." He laughs darkly. "Things that would send you running."

"Show me."

"You don't know what you're asking, little bird."

"I trust you, Luca."

The air sizzles around us. He stares at me a moment longer before nodding, as if he's decided something.

"Fine."

Reaching down, he scoops me into his arms. I'm not sure I'll ever get used to him carrying me like I weigh nothing. His words might have been filled with dark meaning, but there's only fire and heat coming off him now. There's a shift in the air when he carries me to the bed, laying me out before him. My skin prickles with awareness as he moves over me, his lips brushing against mine in the softest kiss. I groan in frustration, and he has the nerve to smile.

"Patience, little bird."

He kisses a trail down my body. When he reaches my

breasts, he laps at my nipple until I'm whimpering. Just when I think I can take no more, he switches to the other one. Over and over, he brings me closer to the edge, but never lets me find release. My body is feverish as he kisses a trail lower.

"Luca, please."

"Please what?"

"Please let me come."

He chuckles. "Not yet."

"Why?"

"You haven't begged yet."

"Please let me come, Luca! I'll do anything!"

He's silent as he parts my folds, blowing cool air across them. I moan, arching into him, but he doesn't give me what I need.

"Damn you!"

"Oh, my sweet little bird, that's definitely not going to make me move any faster." He rolls my clit between his fingers. "Do you want to know what I was doing today when I got cut?"

I nod, unable to think properly as he brings me higher and higher.

"I was killing a man who works for someone out to get me."

I feel like cold water has been dumped on me. "Are you going to be okay?"

"Concerned for me?"

"Yes, I am. I shouldn't be, but I am."

He rewards me with a lick through my folds that ends with him sucking on my clit as I rock against his face.

"Yes, Luca. Like that! Please! I'm so close."

But he pulls back.

"To answer your question, I'm going to be fine. No one

fucks with the Di Bello Family and lives to talk about it." He pauses. "I killed your father for what he did to you. Does that bother you?"

Lord knows I should push him off me, but I don't.

"No."

"No? And why is that?"

"He's a terrible person. He deserved what he got."

"I'm a terrible person, too. I bought you, remember? I took you from your siblings and I'm going to kill you."

"But you haven't killed me yet. By buying me, you saved me and my siblings. As for taking me from them, there's always time to rectify that mistake."

We stare at each other, and I'm certain I've gone too far. This is Luca 'the Beast' Di Bello. No one in their right mind would even think to suggest that he made a mistake.

He shakes his head and moves over me.

"Not going to kill me for that comment?"

"Careful, little bird, or I might just have to spear you to death."

He enters me, and we both groan. I can't stop the smile from spreading across my face. He made a joke. I wonder if he even realizes.

"I like it when you smile," he says.

"And I like it when you spear me like this."

He might like my smile, but I love seeing his. He looks like a different person as his face lights up. Someone who is younger and carefree. Someone I could love. It hits me that this isn't fucking. No, we're making love. My breath hitches in my throat and I pull him closer, seeking his lips. Our kiss is languid, making me more confused that I was before. I'm supposed to hate him. I'm supposed to fear him. I'm not supposed to be falling for him.

"Luca, please make me come," I beg.

He rewards me with another smile and then does just what I've asked. My pleasure builds higher and higher until I leap over the edge into blinding bliss. Luca Di Bello thinks he's dangerous, but the only danger I'm in right now is that he's going to realize that I'm in love with him.

# 15

*Luca*

I wake up with Dove wrapped around me. Fucking hell. Quietly, I move away from her. Maurice stands in the doorway, frozen. That must be what woke me. Glancing at the clock, I see that not only did I sleep in, but I've missed several meetings. Maurice probably didn't even know I was still in the house. Padding naked to the closet, I try to gather my thoughts. What in the fuck happened? I let her sleep with me in my fucking bed. Not only that, but I feel more rested than I've ever felt in my entire life. Rubbing my hand over my face, I groan. Last night was a mistake. So why does it sour my stomach to think that?

After dressing, I motion for Maurice to follow me. He looks back at Dove before setting her tray on the nightstand and following me. We're silent as we make our way to my office on the first floor. I crave a fucking drink, but I don't want to appear weak. So, I settle behind the desk and open my laptop.

"The birdie was out of her cage all night?"

I grunt in response and refuse to meet his gaze.

"Fascinating."

This time I do look up. He's staring at me like I'm one of his experiments waiting to be dissected.

"What?"

His eyebrows lift. "What do you mean?"

"You've clearly got something rattling around in that enormous head of yours."

"You never want to hear what I have to say."

"Well, *Brain*, I figured you could offer some wisdom here."

"You will not like it."

I glare, and it's enough to get him to spit out what's on his mind.

"You've had sex with her, but you've also talked to her, which means she's different from the others. I think you're not sure what you want to do with her. I think the thought of killing her makes you as sick as I was when Grandfather made me kill my parakeet."

*Damn.*

But he's not finished.

"Now you're in this place where you don't know what to do, and that's unlike you. Grandfather would say you're weak. I say you're growing. I think you should let Henri see her. And I think you should try to do something that would make Grandfather angry if he were still alive."

"Like what?"

"Like letting her out of the cage for more than just a night and giving her a chance to get to know the real you."

The real me. That's a laughable statement. I don't know if anyone knows the real me.

Maurice stands. "I'm going to my lab."

He acts like he hasn't just shifted my entire world with

his statement. It also seems like this is something that he's thought about.

"Wait. I've seen you watching her. Maybe you're saying I should free her just so you can get close to her."

He smiles, but it doesn't reach his eyes. "I'm unlovable, Luca, or have you forgotten?"

I sit back in my chair as he walks away like he just didn't gut me. Those were my words that he just threw in my face. Something I said when we were ten years old, because I knew it would please Grandfather. Now? Now I wish I could take them back.

"Fuck."

Reaching for my phone, I send Henri a text. Maurice has always thought I was better than I am. I might not be able to take back what I've done, but I can try to make Dove happy. And that means letting Henri see her. There are other things I need to look at, too. I send Mrs. Lansbury a text next. I've been avoiding her, but now it's time to hear how little Chip and Belle are doing. I might not be able to right all the wrongs in my life, but this is something I can do. All I can do is pray it's enough for Dove to see the real me.

*Dove*

I wake up because my stomach rumbles. Opening my eyes, I'm shocked to find that I'm still in Luca's bed. My tray sits on the nightstand, which means both Luca and Maurice know that I'm out of the cage. Is that a good thing or not?

The door opens and Luca enters. My cheeks feel warm as I smile at him. He doesn't smile. What's made him act this way?

"Good morning."

He goes to the closet, coming out with a dark robe. "Get dressed. There's something I'd like to show you."

I take the robe, slipping it on. My body aches in the best way possible, but it's hard to focus on that when he looks almost ill.

"Has something happened?"

"Come."

We leave the room and go to the first floor. I'm trying not to be worried, but it's hard when he's not speaking. Luca leads the way, opening a door. I'm surprised to find that we're in a small library. It's not as imposing as the library I was taken to the first night here. This one is done in softer tones of sage green that offset the wooden floors. A floral print couch sits next the fireplace. There's a table with a fresh pot of tea and a tray with cookies. I glance at Luca, who motions for me to sit.

Tightening the belt on the robe, I sit. The cushions are soft—the softest thing I've sat on in a long time. A sigh escapes my lips, but I don't think Luca even notices. He busies himself pouring two cups of tea.

"Sugar?"

"Yes, please."

He adds two cubes of sugar and slides the cup and saucer my way. A nervous laugh leaves my lips before I can stop it, and he pauses as if I've insulted him.

"Sorry. I don't think I've ever had tea like this before."

"It's been a while since I've served someone." His lips lift in a small smile. "My grandfather thought it was an important skill to know, though, off the top of my head, I can only think of a handful of times that I've actually used it."

I take a sip of the tea. It's not terrible, though I think I still prefer iced tea.

"It's nice. Thank you."

We sit there in mostly awkward silence. I still can't figure out what's going on. Things have been going so well, but I can't help but fear the other shoe is about to drop. Is he going to give me tea and then kill me? That thought has me setting down the cup.

I'm about to speak when the door opens. Henri strolls in like a man on a mission, coming right to me. I jump to my feet as he pulls me into his embrace.

"Thank fucking god you're safe."

I don't realize I'm crying until he wipes my cheeks.

"It's okay, sweetheart. I'm here."

Luca clears his throat. "I'll give the two of you some privacy." To Henri, he says, "Remember our agreement."

Henri nods, though he is so tense that a vein pops out on his neck.

When the door closes, I ask, "What agreement?"

"I don't want to talk about that right now. Let me look at you."

He leads me to the window, where I feel the sunlight on my skin for the first time in longer than I can remember.

"Is he going to kill me? Is that why you're here?"

"What? No!" He pulls me into his embrace. "I'm not sure what's on his mind. He reached out to me and said he wanted me to come over today. That we need to talk once I've seen you."

"And the agreement?"

"That I won't try to blow his fucking face off the moment I see him."

I snort. "He must get that a lot."

"How has he treated you?"

My cheeks feel warm. How on earth do I tell Henri about what we've been doing? Will he be mad? I decide to go with the truth. They are cousins, and he might know if I'm lying the same way Luca knows.

"Things were rough at first. Scary. I thought I was going to die every day."

"And now?"

"Things have changed." I bite my bottom lip. "We've been spending time together. At night."

"I see."

I reach for him. "Please don't be mad at me."

"I'm not mad. I'm just sorry that I couldn't protect you from him."

"Henri, you did your best."

"But it wasn't enough, was it?" He sighs. "I'm just glad that you're alive. I've been worried sick and when he called, I thought the worst. But something has changed with him."

"What do you mean?"

He motions for me to sit on the couch, and so I do.

"You know there have been others before you, right?"

I nod.

"In the past, we'd have the hunt. If Luca won, he'd take his prize back here, fuck them and then kill them in that order every single time. There was no going back for seconds, and he certainly didn't let them out of the cage."

My chest is tight. "What do you think that means?"

"You're special, Dove. I knew that the moment I saw you. I think Luca sees it, too."

"I'm not special. Luca said that your grandfather taught you how to look for people like me. People who were broken, but who would run when you gave chase. The prey to your predator."

"That much is true. Do you remember the day we met?"

"Of course I do."

"You were startled by something. When I approached the door, I could feel the fear rolling off you. It called to me, but there was also something more." He smiles. "When I saw the state you were in the next day, it hit me you were different. A predator doesn't care if the prey is hurt. I cared. I still care. If I were a betting man, I'd say Luca cares, too."

"So, what happens now?"

He says, "That part is sadly up to Luca. But I think that you're getting through to him. Something no one else has ever done before."

"I saw the cut on his side. He said someone was coming after him and the Di Bello Family. Does it have something to do with that?"

"He told you that?" He whistles. "Wow. I'm speechless."

My cheeks warm and he pats my thigh.

"This is good, Dove. Promising, really."

"I'm going to take your word for it."

He smiles, and I lean into him. God, I've missed him. We spend the next few hours talking about any and everything. He makes sure we're touching at all times, whether it be a hand on my leg or an arm around my shoulder.

"Why do they call you the Brute?"

He snorts. "Grandfather and his sense of humor. He used to say Mo was the Brains, which is true. Luca and his temperament made him the Beast. And I, the willfully strong grandson who wouldn't bow to his every whim, was called the Brute. I don't think he meant it in a good way, but I'd like to think I've made it work for me."

"I'd say you have."

"I'm sorry you had to see me like that. The chase..." he shakes his head. "I shouldn't have taken you in the field like a fucking animal."

My cheeks feel warm. "Does it make me a bad person if I admit that I liked seeing that side of you?"

His gaze searches mine. "Really? You're not just saying that to make me feel better?"

"I truly mean it. There's something in your blood that makes you like the chase. Well, I'm the same because I enjoy being chased." I cup his cheek. "And I'm so glad you were my first."

Leaning forward, his lips brush against mine. It's startling how different his kiss feels after kissing Luca for all this time. The thing that surprises me the most is how I wonder what Maurice's kiss would feel like.

Henri pulls back with a sigh. "I should find Luca. See what he's got on his mind."

"Will you be back?"

"I'm going to try my best."

He leaves me sitting in the room. My eyes water and I swipe at them. Before I have too long to feel sorry for myself, the door opens, and Maurice enters.

"Come on, birdie. Luca has a surprise planned for you."

"For me?"

He nods excitedly.

"Where is Luca now?"

"He's with Ri. I'm glad he asked Ri over."

"I am, too."

I follow him back to Luca's room. On the bed are clothes. Real, actual clothes.

"Luca said to shower and get dressed. You have one hour before we need to leave."

"Where are we going?"

"It's a surprise," he says, as if I didn't hear him the first time.

"Right. Are you coming with me?"

He nods. "But we can't go until you shower. You smell like Luca."

My face flames, but I don't think he notices. He leaves, closing the door behind him. The clothes are things I would usually wear. Jeans, a nice top, and comfortable shoes. All new, with tags, and all in my size. The bra and panties have me smiling. I never thought I'd miss wearing a bra, but being forced to go without one has been a lot. I'm smiling as I go to the bathroom to shower. Again, I find myself surprised. There's a razor, make-up, and hair products. How did he have time to pull this off? And why?

One hour later, I open the door of the bedroom and find Maurice waiting.

"You look so pretty, birdie."

"Thank you, Maurice."

"Let's go."

He leads me to the first floor and right outside. The ground is covered in snow, and I should probably ask for a coat, but I don't. Instead, I pause in the doorway.

"What's wrong?"

"Are you sure this is okay?"

He nods. "Positive."

"Maurice, I really don't want to make Luca mad."

"I won't be mad," Luca says from behind me.

Henri is at his side. I wish I knew him better so I could tell what the look on his face meant. He does give me a small nod, which is better than nothing. I don't think he'd let me leave if Luca was going to kill me. At least, I hope not.

Luca says, "Enjoy your day. There will be another surprise when you get home."

"Not afraid I'm going to ask for help while I'm out?"

I meant it teasingly, but it comes out more serious.

"I can't stop you. All I can do is ask that you give me a chance."

Why does it feel like he's asking for so much more? And why do I want to say yes? Turning, I follow Maurice outside to the waiting SUV. He opens the back door for me before getting into the driver's seat. We pull away from the house, the tires crunching in the snow.

"Is it crazy that I'm scared?"

I don't expect him to answer, but I just need to talk.

He says, "Don't be scared, birdie. I won't let anything hurt you."

"Why do you call me birdie?"

"Because that's what you are. A dove. I had a birdie before. She was pretty, just like you."

"What was her name?"

"Merry Christmas, but I called her MC for short. She was a parakeet."

"What happened to her?"

"Grandfather made me kill her. Said that if I didn't, he would kill Ri." His gaze meets mine. "I was scared, too."

"Maurice…"

"Don't be sorry for me, birdie. I was glad to save Ri, just like I'm glad to save you."

He turns his attention back to the road and is silent as we drive into Chicago. I've missed the hustle and bustle of the city. Holiday decorations line the light poles and storefronts, meaning I've been gone for around two months now. Am I crazy for falling for Luca and Henri in such a short amount of time? I just don't know anymore, which could be a form of Stockholm Syndrome.

The SUV comes to a stop in front of a trendy restaurant, which usually has lines out the door.

"Why are we here?"

Maurice doesn't answer, but says, "I'll be waiting out here when you're ready to go home."

Two months ago, home would have been a tiny apartment. Now I'm not sure... Is Luca's house my home? It feels like it, even inside the cage. Shaking my head, I exit the SUV. Time to see what kind of surprise Luca has in store for me.

# 16

*Dove*

The restaurant is empty, except for three women who sit around a round table. The dark headed one with grey eyes stands, smiling.

"You must be Dove. I'm Amelia Hook. This is Winter Phrygia and Goldie Behr."

I'm shocked. These women are married to the most powerful men in the city. I've read all about them in the paper. And, if memory serves me, Amelia made national news when her uncle-by-marriage kidnapped her. What on earth are they doing here?

"Please, sit."

I take the chair between her and Winter.

Winter smiles. "It's nice to meet you. We all wondered when Luca would let you out of your cage."

The others laugh, but my breath hitches in my throat. Does everyone know how I've been living, or was it just an expression that's oddly specific in my case?

Goldie meets my gaze across the table. "Are you okay, Dove? You look pale."

The others turn my way, staring at me. I feel sick. My mouth opens, but no words come out. Where do I even start?

Goldie says, "I know meeting everyone can be a lot, but I promise we're harmless." Her lips lift in a small smile. "Unless we're dealing with human traffickers, that is."

"Traffickers?" I echo.

She nods, her blonde curls bouncing. "Yeah. We recently discovered that some women working at my husbands' brothel were purchased at a human auction. Since then, we've been working with a woman down in Georgia to end trafficking in the states. Or, at least, shut down the bigger operations."

"Did you say husbands?"

Everyone around the table giggles.

"Yeah. I'm legally married to Atticus, but his foster brothers and I are also together." She rubs her rounded stomach. "There's a bet right now on who the father is. Honestly, I plan to give each of them a kid, so it doesn't matter."

She doesn't act like it's odd that she has more than one partner. My mind goes from Luca to Henri to Maurice, and I pause. I guess it might not be that strange.

Amelia says, "You'll find that each of us has more than one partner. I'm married to Hook, but I'm also with Smee and Ronan…"

There's something sad in her gaze that makes my heart ache, and I'm not sure why.

She shakes her head. "Sorry. My hormones are still all over the place since having the babies."

"Don't be sorry. How old are they?"

"Two months old today, and I'm missing them like crazy."

"I was the same way when I had to leave my little sister, Belle, for the first time."

Amelia asks, "You take care of your sister?"

"And brother."

"That's great. I recently adopted my younger cousins."

Goldie grins. "Tell her how many kids you have now."

Amelia doesn't look the least bit embarrassed as she says, "Six, and we hope to add to our family as soon as we can."

Winter, who's been mostly quiet until now, says, "Lord, you'll have enough kids to make up for the ones I *don't* want to have."

"You don't want kids?"

She shakes her head. "Nope. Even had the surgery to make sure there aren't any accidents. What about you? Should we be expecting a little Luca Di Bello running around soon?"

"God, I hope not." They laugh and I cover my face. "That didn't come out the way I meant it to."

"That rough, huh?" Winter smiles. "If it makes you feel any better, my husband literally kidnapped and tortured me when we first met. And that was after his second-in-command took a side job to kill me. Obviously, he didn't go through with it, but definitely made for a rough time until we finally fucked it out."

I laugh at her bluntness.

Amelia adds, "You'll find that we all came to be with our men in unusual ways. Mine kidnapped me, too."

Goldie says, "And I broke into my guys' house, where they caught me. What about you?"

They each seem genuine, as if I can talk to them and they won't judge me.

"My father sold me to pay off a debt."

Goldie scowls. "Creep."

"Luca was the one who bought me and made me take part in a chase." My cheeks warm and I rush on. "I had to run from him, Henri, and Maurice. Run for my life, to be exact. And now things are... complicated."

Goldie grins. "Girl, we love complicated around here. Let me guess. You're having feeling for one or more of them and aren't sure if it's real or maybe because you've been kidnapped and are now fucked in the head."

"Yeah, that sums it up perfectly."

"Listen, no one knows what it's like to be in our shoes. We each hold the attention of the most powerful men in the city. It's a lot, right?" At my nod, she continues, "But you still know your heart. If you're feeling something, then it's likely real."

Amelia adds, "But if it's not, we can help you."

"Help me how?"

"We can get you away from the Di Bello Family and give you time to think."

It's everything I thought I wanted. Except, now that it's within my reach, I'm not sure what to do.

Winter touches my arm. "Dove, there's nothing wrong with wanting to stay. If you knew the things Midas did to me, you would ask if I'm in my right mind because I stayed. And I would do it all over again to be with him, Doc, Huntsman, and Blick."

"Thanks. That's somehow helpful."

Amelia says, "Let's order some food and you can tell us more about you. I have a feeling we're going to be seeing a lot of you."

By the time lunch is over, I feel more like myself than I have in months. More importantly than that, I know I don't want to leave Luca's house. Not until we have time to talk. Each of my new friends promise to see me soon, and I believe them. Maurice is waiting outside and smiles when he sees me. He opens the back door of the SUV, but I stop him by throwing my arms around his neck.

"Thank you, Maurice."

His cheeks are red as he answers, "This wasn't me. This was Luca."

"I don't believe you. I think you have this way of getting to people, and that you somehow convinced Luca to show me a different side of him."

"Only because you deserve more than a pretty cage, birdie."

I brush my lips across his cheeks. "And you deserve more than to hide in the shadows, Maurice."

He doesn't answer, but motions for me to climb into the SUV. When I'm inside, he closes the door and takes his place in the driver's seat.

"Where are we going now?"

"Home."

"Do you live there all the time as well? I always just assumed the Beast needed to be in the city."

"We each live in the city, but all of us consider Grandfather's home our true home."

I see his scowl in the mirror.

"You should try to make new memories there. Things that will make it a happy home."

This time, he looks at me. "That's what I'm hoping you can help us do."

I sit back, stunned. It never crossed my mind that I could help these men. They hold so much power and I'm a nobody. But the thought of helping them does something to my heart. I want each of them to be happy. To know there are other ways to live than what they were taught. So, I decide to make it my mission to show them how it might be if they give me a chance.

We arrive at the house, and both Luca and Henri are waiting. It doesn't look like there's been bloodshed, so that's a plus.

Henri meets me, pulling me into his arms. "Did you have a good time?"

I look up at him, searching his face. "I did. Is everything okay here?"

"Yes. But I think Luca should be the one to explain."

Luca scowls at that. "I'm sure you can do it better, *professor*."

Henri chuckles, unphased by the slight dig. "No, this is your idea. You should tell her."

"Tell me what?"

Luca sighs. "Come inside. It's quite cold out here."

I follow him into the house, Henri right behind me. Glancing over my shoulder, I see Maurice is following, too. Good. I'm led to another room that I've never been to. This one is more like a den and is definitely more comfortable. The brown leather couches face a fireplace with a TV hanging over it. There's a minibar, too, which I think must be some kind of prerequisite for this family. Luca motions for me to sit. I'm pleased when Henri sits at my side, so close that our bodies touch. Maurice takes a seat on the loveseat and Luca stands. He stares into the fireplace, lost in his thoughts.

"Luca?"

He blinks, facing me. "Right. Did you have a good time today?"

"I already asked her that," Henri reminds him.

He glares, his cheeks darkening in a blush.

"Luca, is everything okay?"

"I guess that depends on how you feel once you hear what I have to say."

I nod. "Okay."

"I think we're all aware of what my plan was when I brought you here. I was going to do what I was trained to do. The same thing I've done a dozen other times before. But there's something different about you, Dove. Something that has me questioning myself for the first time."

Henri snorts. "Cousin, this is going to take all night if you don't get to the fucking point."

"I'm fucking trying."

I've never seen him this agitated. Without thinking, I stand and go to him.

"Luca, you can tell me."

His gaze settles on me. "I'd like to start over. With you. Give you a chance to get to know the real me. But I know you have feelings for Henri, too."

"And Maurice," I say. I want them to know that he's part of this, too, at least for me.

"And Maurice." He rubs his thumb over his bottom lip. "How would you feel about staying here as a guest as we get to know each other?"

"What about the whole killing me thing?"

"You have my word that I will not kill you."

"And if this doesn't work out between us?"

A pained expression flashes across his face. "Then I will let you go, Dove. You have my word."

"What about Chip and Belle?"

He smirks down at me. "I think you should consider

looking into law school when this is over. You have a natural knack for debating and negotiating."

"I might do that. Now, what happens to them?"

"They are at one of my homes out of the city, just like you asked. I've arranged for you to see them when you're ready, though I hope you give our new agreement some time before you go." At my questioning look, he says, "They're not going to want to let you go once they see you. I can't say that I blame them."

"What happens if it works here, with the four of us? Will my brother and sister be welcomed to live with us?"

"Yes."

I exhale. "Well, Beast, I think we have a new agreement then. Shall we kiss on it?"

His eyes widen in surprise before he gives me a devious smile. "I think that sounds like the perfect way to seal this deal."

Lowering his head, he captures my face with his hands and brushes his lips against mine. The kiss starts out soft, but soon turns deep. That's just how everything with Luca seems to go, not that I mind. We kiss until I feel dizzy. When he pulls back, we share a smile.

Henri says, "It's only fair that I seal this deal, too."

"Of course."

He comes to me, kissing me softly. Again, I'm struck at the difference in their kisses. I laugh when he nibbles on my lip.

"I like the playful side of you."

"Good."

Turning, I meet Maurice's gaze. He's watching me with an anguished look on his face that breaks my heart.

"Maurice, I meant what I said. I want to get to know you, too."

He shakes his head, backing from the room.

Luca says, "Don't take it personally. Maurice doesn't let anyone get close to him."

I nod, but I'm not giving up on him. Not at all.

"What happens now?"

Luca says, "Henri can show you your new room and then we can all have dinner together."

"My room. I don't have to stay in the cage."

"Not unless you want to." He holds up his hands. "I'm joking. No, you don't have to stay in there."

"Where is the room?"

"In the east wing."

I shake my head. "I want to stay in the west wing, near your room."

He seems pleased by this. "Then I will make the arrangements."

Henri says, "I can show you the rest of the house while Luca makes that happen."

I don't miss the lingering gaze Luca gives me as I follow Henri from the room. I'm having a hard time wrapping my mind around everything, but Henri is right by my side, letting me know this is really happening. He shows me the entire house and even takes me outside after bundling me in a coat that's too big for me.

"I think I'm going to need a map to get around."

"We can make that happen."

"Henri, what happened after I left this morning?"

He motions for me to sit on a bench after brushing off the snow for me.

"Luca wanted to talk. He basically said the same thing to me that he said to you. He also invited me to stay here with you. Said that I deserve a chance as much as does." He laughs softly. "I'm not sure what kind of spell you put on him, but I've never seen him like this before."

"I don't think it's a spell. I think he's finally seeing that he might not be the person he thought he was. There's goodness inside of him. In all of you, really."

He kisses the top of my head. "I take it back. It's not a spell that you've put on him. It's a fucking miracle."

That has me laughing. "Be nice."

"Anything for you, sweetheart." He stands, holding out his hand. "Let's see if your new room is ready."

"I still can't believe he's letting me have my own room."

"Me, either. It's a whole new Luca."

Hand-in-hand, we make our way inside. Luca is nowhere to be found, and neither is Maurice. On the second floor, we go to the west wing. There's a single door open, and it's in the room next to Luca's. Entering, I smile. It's perfect, as if Luca already knows my style. Of course, he has been watching me, so he likely *does* know. The bedding is airy, reminding me of springtime. The furniture is a deep cherry wood. There's comfortable looking chair sitting on a fuzzy rug that's near the fireplace. The closet is filled with items I would pick to wear on my own, as well as more formal items.

Henri whistles. "Looks like my cousin is planning on you being here for a while."

And I'm okay with that.

I turn to Henri. "Do you think I'm crazy?"

"Crazy? Why would I think that?"

"Because I want to stay here and get to know him."

"Not crazy at all. Smart. Cautious. Wise. But not crazy."

I smile. "Okay."

He tugs me from the closet to the bed. "Let's take a nap before dinner."

I grin. "No Netflix and chill?"

"Oh, we can most definitely do that, too."

Kicking off my shoes, I strip down to my bra and panties and then dive under the covers. He watches me before doing the same. I snuggle against him in the bed as we get comfortable.

Henri cradles me, tracing circles on my arm. "Are you happy?"

"I am." I think back to the sadness in Maurice's eyes as he left earlier. "I just wish Maurice would give me a chance."

"Mo's had a hard life. He's more sensitive than me and Luca and was punished for it. Give him time. He'll come around."

I kiss his chest. "I hope you're right."

"I know my cousin. He likes you."

"Good. Because I like him as much as I like you and Luca." Peering up at him, I ask, "Is it weird that we all might be in a relationship?"

He smiles down at me. "No."

"I was shocked when I met the girls today and found out they're each in relationships with multiple men. It hit me that maybe Luca wanted me to meet them so I could see that it's not so strange."

"That was part of it, for sure. He wanted you to meet them because they are the wives of the most powerful men in the city. You are now with the last unmarried man in that group. Knowing those women will help you."

My cheeks feel warm, and I sit. "Does he want to marry me?"

"Luca always said he'd never get married, but I think you're making him reconsider a lot of things. Does that bother you?"

I shake my head. "No."

"I will pass that along."

Laughing, I playfully punch his shoulder. "Such a mean Daddy."

He groans. "Fuck. I've waited a long time to hear you say that again."

"What? Daddy?"

He nods. "I know the day we messed around; you had been through a lot. I wasn't sure if you were just caught up in the moment or if it's something you're in to."

"Oh, I'm definitely into it. I don't think I've ever been that wet before." I laugh. "And you better not tell Luca that, because he'll prove me wrong."

"My lips are sealed. But only because I've missed my little girl."

"Is that so? Then I have one thing to say." Leaning forward, I nip his ear lobe. "Give me more than the tip this time, Daddy."

# 17

*Dove*

The next three weeks are filled with more happiness than I thought humanly possible. Each day I get to know Luca, Henri, and even Maurice a bit more. My nights are spent with Luca or Henri. We're all at breakfast when I clear my throat.

"Luca, I'm in love with you."

He drops the fork in his hand, and it clatters against his plate.

"What?"

"You heard me. I'm in love with you. Do you love me?"

His eyes are wide, as if he doesn't know what to do with this information. Henri and I have already said we love each other, but I need Luca to know. To see if he feels the same for me.

"I... I—" His phone rings and he glances at the screen. "Fuck. I need to take this."

Grabbing it, he leaves the dining room. My eyes water and Henri reaches for my hand.

"He needed to hear it, Dove."

"Maybe it was too soon."

Maurice asks, "Too soon for what?"

I meet his gaze. "I love each of you and I need you to know so we can start building our lives together."

He, too, is speechless. Fuck. I'm making a mess out of things.

I don't have time to explain myself further because Luca comes back, a serious look on his face.

"Brute, there's been an attack. We need to go. Brain, stay with Dove. We'll be in contact as soon as we know something."

Right before my eyes, they each go into fighting more. These are the men their grandfather raised them to be, which means something terrible has happened.

"Please be safe," I say.

But neither Luca nor Henri answer. They leave a moment later and I can't stop the sense of dread that settles over me.

Maurice says, "Come on, birdie. Let's go to your room and play a card game."

I've learned over the last few weeks that Maurice likes to play cards. Nodding, I follow him to my room.

"Where do you think they went?"

Maurice shuffles the cards and answers, "I'm not sure. They didn't say, but that just means they don't need my brains for this one."

We play several rounds of cards, all while I wait for them to return. When the sun settles into the west, I stand, needing to move. Maurice stands, too.

"Do you want to know a secret, birdie?"

"Yes."

"I was with Luca the first time he saw you. You were on your way to work at the diner and rushed right past us."

"Really? I did not know."

"You were wearing a yellow shirt, the same yellow that my parakeet was. I knew it was a sign. When we found out your name, I knew it was meant to be."

Somehow, I believe the same thing. Nothing in this world happens by chance.

"If it's meant to be, then why won't you let me get close to you?"

He looks at the distance between us as we stand. "We're close now, birdie."

"That's not what I mean. I want to kiss you."

"Not a good idea, birdie."

I move toward him. "Please. Just one kiss."

He shakes his head. "Bad things happen to things I love, birdie. I can't lose you. It would hurt too much."

We're standing chest to chest. I swear I can feel his heart pounding. He's so scared, but he doesn't have to be.

I whisper, "Maurice, please. I'm not going anywhere."

His eyes close as a single tear falls down his cheek. I catch it with my tongue, drinking it away. His sorrow will become mine, if only at this moment. He exhales shakily as I press my lips against his in a soft kiss. When he doesn't push me away, I do it again. And again. Finally, his lips part, welcoming me in. Our kiss starts out slow, but soon consumes both of us as we allow ourselves to *feel*.

"Maurice Di Bello, I think I'm falling for you," I say, caressing his cheek.

His eyes open. "I loved you the moment I first saw you, birdie."

We kiss again, but this time he pulls me close. His kiss makes me feel like I've lived a thousand lives with him before. It's like coming home. It's beautiful and completes me. My eyes water, and I wrap my arms around his neck. Things are going to be okay. Once Luca and Henri get home, I'm going to tell them I want to stay with them forever.

"Maurice," I moan against his lips. "I need you."

He pulls back, looking down at me in awe. "You truly want me, birdie? Even though my head rattles with thoughts that make little sense?"

"Yes."

He pulls me against him in the tightest hug, but I don't mind. I love him, and it's time he knows this.

"Have you ever been with a woman before?"

It's something I've wondered, and I want to make sure he's okay with what I want to do with him.

"I have, though I didn't enjoy it. Grandfather made me..."

"I don't want you to do anything that you're not ready for. We can take this as slow as you want, Maurice. I want you to *want* this."

"I do want this. I want you, birdie." His cheeks are red. "But what if you aren't happy when it's over?"

"Oh, my sweet Maurice, that will not happen. Want to know how I know?" At his nod, I say, "Because you make me happy. This will just add to that happiness.

Moving down, I watch as he strokes himself with one hand. With the other, he pulls me closer until I settle between his thighs. Reaching out, I mimic his own actions until he's rocking into my hand, his deep grunts filling the room. The tip of his cock glistens and I lean forward, licking the juices off, savoring the flavor. He breathes out my name, making me smile.

"Still okay?"

"Better than okay. Feels so good."

That's what I want to hear. I fist him, pumping him as I lick the tip.

"Birdie, I need to be inside of your mouth."

His words send a rush of moisture between my legs, and I nod, opening my mouth. Breathing through my nose, I take him deep into my throat until I gag. Maurice pulls back before thrusting. My throat contracts as I swallow, and he moans.

"Fuck. Birdie, yes. Just like that."

His head tilts back in pleasure. Seeing him like this makes me so horny. I'm making him come undone like this. I'm the only person he's ever wanted in this way, too. Holding onto his thighs, I give him my best, which has him crying out incoherent words before he pulls away from me.

"Wait. I want to do this the right way. In bed."

Not needing to be told twice, I climb onto the bed. He moves over me, and we kiss.

"Are you still okay with this?"

He nods. "If I don't slide into your heat, I just might die, birdie."

I smile. "Well, we don't want that, now do we?

Spreading my legs, I encourage him to position himself at my opening. He runs a finger through my folds.

"You're dripping wet."

"It's because I want you so much, Maurice."

"I'll try to be gentle," he warns. "But I can't promise anything."

"I just want you, baby."

He enters me in a thrust that leaves both of us making sounds of pleasure.

"So, so good," he moans.

We rock against each other as we climb higher and higher.

"Not going to last long," he chants.

I'm not either. Not when I see the wild look in his blue eyes that hurdles me toward my orgasm. Wrapping my legs around his waist, I buck against him until he meets my frantic thrusts. My body is on fire, but it's nothing compared to what I feel when his mouth crashes over mine. My stomach tightens and I gasp against his lips as my entire world goes white with the rush of my release.

"Maurice! Oh, yes," I cry.

His cock jerks inside of me as he comes, too, and we grind against each other in an animalistic heat as I come again. Tears leak from my eyes, and I feel so freaking weak, but he continues to thrust, as if he's scared he'll never feel that kind of pleasure again. My third orgasm leaves my throat burning from all the screaming I'm doing.

Maurice pulls out of me, rubbing my clit. "Come for me, birdie. Show me how alive I make you feel."

Somehow, he drags a fourth orgasm out of me. I cry, biting his shoulder as I ride wave after wave of pleasure. I think I must pass out, because the next time I come to, he's holding me.

"Did I hurt you, birdie?"

I stretch next to him. "God, no. That was perfect, Maurice." I kiss his hand. "I never thought I could be this happy."

"Me, too." He smiles, looking up at the ceiling. "Birdie, you made my heart sing tonight."

"You made mine sing, too. I know it's probably too soon to say this, but I love you."

His eyes widen as he looks at me. "Birdie..."

"You don't have to say it back. Just know that I do love you as much as I love Henri and Luca." I snuggle against him. "When they get back, I want to tell them, too."

"I'd like that."

We settle into a comfortable silence, half dozing in post-coital bliss. Just when I'm about to suggest another round of love making, there's a loud crash from downstairs. Maurice bolts from the bed, reaching for his clothes. I do the same, my heart pounding wildly.

"Is it Luca? Have they returned?"

He shakes his head. "It's not them. Come on. We need to get to the first floor, to the safe room."

Taking me by the hand, he leads me to the hallway, where he presses a panel on the wall. It swings open, revealing a hidden stairway.

"Down we go. Be careful, birdie."

I follow him, fear coursing through me. We reach the bottom of the stairs and Maurice opens a small peephole. When he's sure the coast is clear, he opens the door. We're in Luca's study. I haven't been in this room since the first day that I was brought here. Being here feels like a bad omen.

"Maurice..."

There's another crash in the hallway, and it sounds close. And then I hear voices. Men. And a lot of them. Are these people the ones Luca mentioned? The ones out to get him? If so, does that mean they already got to Luca and Henri? Is that why Luca left in a rush?

The doorknob jiggles. "I bet they're in here. Monsieur said there were safe rooms and hidden passages throughout the house."

I meet Maurice's gaze. His eyes are wild with fear.

"Dove, hide."

The use of my real name sends terror coursing through my body.

"I'm not going to leave you here!"

He grabs me by the hand, pulling me across the room to

another panel on the wall. It swings open, and he pushes me inside, closing the panel behind me. I'm in some kind of space that's the size of a closet but is empty. I hold my breath as footsteps approach.

"Maurice. What a pleasant surprise. Of course, we already know that Luca and Henri are out of the house." There's a pause. "Monsieur D'Arque sent a message that they couldn't refuse."

Another voice adds, "Using small children as bait often has that outcome. A trick learned from George Peters."

Small children? Do they have Chip or Belle? I think back to the look on Henri's face as they left. He was upset, but I didn't think too much about it. Oh, my god. What if something happened to Chip or Belle?

"The Beast really messed up when he went against us."

Maurice says, "If you have an issue with him, you need to speak to him directly. I'm not his mouthpiece."

"That's not what we heard. Word around the street is that you're the man we need to see to make a point." The man laughs. "The only thing better would be if the bitch was here, too."

An unknown voice says, "Her father said she was easy. I guess it's true since I've seen the photos of her with the Beast and the Brute. Tell us, Brain, have you had her, too?"

Maurice answers in a monotone voice, "I am unlovable."

"No shit. We heard what happened to your mom. No wonder you're so fucked in the head."

Rage courses through me. How dare they taunt Maurice like that!

Maurice's voice is further away as he says, "You should leave. Once the Beast finds out that the D'Arque Family was here, he'll make sure you pay."

"Oh, we're counting on it. And that's why you're coming with us."

"I'm not going anywhere with you."

"That's where you're wrong, you freak. You're coming and once we get you to the asylum, we're going to show you what we would have done to you if you had been born into our family."

My eyes fill with tears as the sound of a fist meeting flesh fills the air. There's a deep grunt and then nothing.

"Pick him up. We need to get out of here before the Beast returns." There's a pause. "And the woman? Did you find her?"

"No, she's hidden somewhere. It's okay. This will be enough to draw them out."

The thing is, I know these men are right. When they return, they're going to do whatever it takes to get Maurice back. And I'm going to help them.

I'm not sure how long I stand in the hidden room. Long enough that my feet ache and I sit on the floor. That's where I am when the panel opens, and Luca looks down at me.

"Thank fucking god." He pulls me to my feet, hugging me close.

"They have Maurice," I cry. "They said they were taking him to the asylum! They're going to hurt him. We have to go!"

Luca holds me closer. "We're going to get him, little bird. I swear it. But you have to stay here."

"I can't. I need to be there with you."

"D'Arque had Chip and Belle. They're here. Chip is upset. He could really use his big sister."

"Chip and Belle are here? Were they hurt?"

Henri answers, "They aren't hurt, but they're scared."

I'm torn. I want to make sure Chip and Belle are truly

okay, but I will never forgive myself if something happens to Maurice.

"I'm going with you. Once we have Maurice, the four of us can come home. Is there someone to watch the kids?"

Luca nods. "We found Mrs. Lansbury tied up in the nursery. She's here, too, looking after the kids."

"Good. Let's go."

"You need to change first, little bird."

I look down at my night clothes, realizing he's right.

"Come with me. I don't want you to leave without me."

His lips lift in a small smile, but he follows me to his room where he helps me pick out all black clothes. Even though I have clothes in my own closet, he keeps some in here, too. When this is over, I'm going to tell him that I want the four of us to share one room. I need them to be as close as possible, and so multiple rooms just aren't going to work for me anymore.

"To help us blend in," Luca explains as he changes his own shirt to a black one.

"What is the asylum?"

"It's exactly what you would think it is. Back in the 1800s, it's where the mentally unstable were sent. Terrible things happened to them there. It closed in 1960. That's when the D'Arque family bought it."

"They mentioned a Monsieur D'Arque. Who is he?"

"Guillaume D'Arque is the head of their family. He's the one I mentioned who thinks he can go against me and win."

And now he has Maurice.

"Will D'Arque kill Maurice?"

"I don't know," he admits.

I nod. "Let's go get our guy."

## 18

*Maurice*

Pain.

All I feel is pain.

My thoughts are jumbled, making it hard for me to know what's really happening. Is Grandfather back? He likes this kind of treatment. Always saying that I don't belong. That I'm a disappointment to the Di Bello family. He's right. I shouldn't be a Di Bello. But here I am.

I'm suspended by my arms, my feet barely touching the ground. When they hit me just right, I spin like a piñata on a rope, but candy won't fall from me, no matter how hard they hit me. The thought makes me cough out a laugh.

"Can you believe this freak? He hasn't made a fucking sound and yet he's *laughing*."

Another man answers, "Maybe you just don't hit as hard as you think. Let me try."

More pain. More jumbled thoughts. All I see is Dove's face. She's safe. That's all that matters. My sweet birdie. I won't let her life end because of me, and she won't end up in a box buried deep in the ground like my parakeet.

"Monsieur D'Arque is coming. He'll get a reaction out of the freak. No one can withstand his punishment."

Guillaume D'Arque is here? That's good. That means he didn't hurt Luca or Ri. It also means I'm going to die, but that's something I can make peace with. Dove showed me what it felt like to be loved. Even now, I feel the warmth of her deep in my heart. The only way they can take that away is if they cut my heart out, just like George Peters did to Ivan Rackham. A death I'm willing to die if it means my birdie is safe.

"What do we have here?"

D'Arque. I'd recognize his nasal voice anywhere. He thinks he sounds so fancy with a French accent, but everyone knows it's fake. Just like he is. One day, Luca and Ri will show him what actual power looks like. And I will smile down from the heavens above.

"Look at me, Maurice."

I open my good eye. D'Arque stands before me, smiling.

"You've done well, but it's time to give up. I need something to send the Beast, and a body part from you will get the point across that I mean business." He smirks at me. "Unless you want to tell me where to find the woman. Dove, I think, is her name."

He moves closer to me, taunting me. He's so focused that he doesn't expect the headbutt that knocks him backward. Fiery pleasure courses through me. I'm going to pay for that, but it was worth it.

"Stupid, stupid man."

D'Arque snaps his fingers and I brace myself. This piñata is about to break. I know it deep in my soul.

Pain.

So much pain.

There's a wetness on my face that I know comes from blood, but I don't care.

Dove is safe.

My birdie is safe.

Safe.

That's all I ever wanted.

I hear a scream. Opening my eyes, I know I must be dead because Dove is standing there like an angel. She's talking, but I don't hear a word she's saying. A bright light calls to me, welcoming me to a place where I can finally rest. And I'm so exhausted, so I should follow it. See how Ivan is doing. I always liked him.

"Goodbye, birdie."

# 19

*DiBello*

*Dove*

*"Goodbye, birdie."*

The words are barely a whisper, but I hear them as if Maurice screamed them. His eyes close, and his body goes limp. Rushing past Luca, I go to his side, trying to get him down. He's hanging from some kind of hook that's too tall for me to reach.

"Dove!"

I turn as a fist makes contact with my face, knocking me to the ground. I've been hit before, but never like this. Looking up, I find a man towering over me.

"You must be the bitch that I've been looking for. Let me introduce myself. I'm Guillaume D'Arque, but you may call me Master from this day forward."

My father used to say I never knew when to keep my mouth shut, and now is one of those moments.

I laugh. "Anyone ever tell you that you resemble a walking penis? Scrotum and all?

Someone coughs to cover a laugh, and it's enough to make him strike me again.

Shoving myself to my feet, I say, "That's the last hit you're going to get, buddy."

"And what makes you think that? As far as I can tell, you're outnumbered. It's you, two men, and a dead guy."

My heart lurches in my chest. Maurice isn't dead. He can't be!

He continues, "My men and I outnumber you tenfold, at least."

I smile. "And that's why you'll always be second best."

Moving away from him, he can now see the red beams trained at the center of his chest. The same thing happens to every man around the room. Crossing the room, I stand next to Henri and Luca.

"When we left the house, Luca and Henri were going over the plan of attack. It was a good plan, too, but then I reminded them of something. Want to know what it is?"

He spits out, "What?"

"We are one of the most powerful families in the city. We are too important to deal with scum like you. So, I encouraged my guys to give some friends a call. Friends who happily came when we said we needed help."

The door on the opposite side of the room opens and Hook walks in with Smee and Ronan. Above us, on the second floor, Midas, Doc, Huntsman, and Blick appear at the railing. And behind us, the three Behr brothers enter. Guillaume D'Arque visibly pales, and it makes me so fucking happy.

"I'd tell you to give up, but it won't make a difference. We've decided the city is better without scum like you, so you and your men won't be walking out of here."

Henri and Luca move past me, going to Maurice. Once

they have him down, we walk out of the warehouse as all hell breaks loose. I'm only focused on Maurice.

"Is he okay?"

"I'm still here, birdie."

His eyes open, and I exhale. "Thank god."

Henri says, "You gave us a good scare, Mo."

"Sorry, Ri."

Suddenly, every emotion that I've shoved down over the past few hours escapes as I sob into my hands. Someone puts an arm around me, pulling me close.

"I was so scared," I finally say, looking up. "I'm in love with each of you. I can't lose you now."

Luca, who I discover is the one holding me, says, "We love you, too, little bird."

"Do you mean it? You love me?"

"I do."

Maurice adds, "I do, too."

Henri smiles. "You already know how I feel."

Nodding, I let out another sob. "Here's what's going to happen. I want to go home and see my siblings. Then I want to move into Luca's room, but it's not just going to be me. All four of us are going to share the room. Understand?"

They are all silent, and someone clears their throat behind me. Turning, I see Hook standing there.

He says, "It's finished. Guillaume D'Arque and his family are no longer an issue for us or for the city of Chicago."

Luca nods. "Thank you."

"I suggest you do what your lovely woman suggests. Go home and enjoy yourselves. We can handle the rest. Midas has already sent for the chainsaws."

My stomach roils at the thought, but I try to remain

stoic, so the guys don't worry. Henri and Luca help Maurice to his feet, and Hook motions me over.

"Can I offer you some advice?"

"Sure."

His tone lowers. "Amelia always gets extra... *sensitive* when she's in her first trimester. Any and everything makes her cry, and her moods are all over the place."

I'm speechless as I try to calculate when my last period was. Holy mother of god. Am I pregnant?

Hook pats my arm. "Might want to get a test on your way home. You know, just in case. And know that Amelia and Goldie can both offer you guidance, if that's the case."

"Thank you."

"No, thank you. I've hoped that Luca would see that the three Families could work together for a long time. You have brought us together, which makes the city even stronger."

My cheeks are warm as he leaves.

Luca joins my side. "What was that about?"

"He was just thanking me for bringing you all together."

He grunts, but it's not nearly as vicious as it once was.

"Let's go home, little bird. We have the rest of our lives to start."

# EPILOGUE

*DiBelle*

*Luca*
*\*\*\*New Year's Eve\*\*\**

I fucking hate parties, but Dove wanted to be here. She's with the other wives, and I'm pleased to see how the rose ring on her left ring finger catches the light. I asked her to marry me on Christmas Day, and she said yes. Of course, Henri had to one-up me and ask her, too. Maurice said he was okay just having her in his life, but I know my girl. She's going to want a wedding with the three of us. And I'll do it because I fucking love her.

Chip is playing with Amelia and Hook's sons, Junior, Robert, Michael, and Theodore. He's closest in age to Michael, but all of them get along. Baby Belle is in the nursery with little Eloise and her twin brother, Ivan. The Hook family, who is hosting tonight's party, graciously offered for Chip and Belle to stay the night so that we can celebrate our engagement. Got to say, Hook has turned out to be a real fucking gem. They all have, to be honest.

Goldie, who looks ready to burst, groans. "Fuck. I think my water just broke!"

Atticus, Oliver, and Finn rush to her side, looking frantic. I've never seen the big, bad Behr brothers look so scared. Winter goes to their side, telling them what they need to do. The room is pure chaos, but that's just how life is these days.

Midas and Huntsman choose this moment to join me.

"Big things are happening out in New York City."

I turn to Midas. "Anything we need to know about?"

"Elsa is retiring. She's taking our lead and has already picked her replacements."

That has me snorting. "Guess she didn't get the memo that it would be easier to just give the key to the kingdom to one Family."

I'm joking, and he knows it. In the past, I would have meant the words. Now I see the beauty in sharing the burden with those that you can trust.

"Guess not." He looks me in the eyes. "I've hinted that Malik Jafar should call you. You two are very... similar in more ways than one. I think you can offer him guidance that no one else can."

"I'm touched, but I'm not interested in babysitting, especially someone with the reputation that Jafar has."

Huntsman snorts. "That's rich coming from you, Di Bello."

Midas says, "Think about it, Luca. They're going to need our help. Hook and Company have already reached out to Kieran Van der Zee. I believe the Behr brothers are in talks with Odin Vilulf."

Dove and Henri join the conversation. Dove must have heard enough because she has a determined look on her face.

She touches my arm. "Jafar runs several hotels in New

York City. We can show him how we're doing things here. Show him that thinking outside of the box can work."

I don't miss Henri smirking. He knows she's got me.

"You're right, little bird." To Midas, I say, "I'll reach out."

"Thank you."

"Never thought I'd live to see the day that you would thank me."

"Don't let it go to your head. The day is young and you're likely to piss me off before it's said and done with."

We share a smile. It's strange. I used to hate being in the position I'm in. I thought Midas had done me a disservice by not leaving me in charge. As much as I bitch and moan, I can see the benefits of having others to share the burden. My gaze goes around the room, taking in the people here. Midas might have picked his successors, but it's the women here who have made us what we are. I can admit that.

Dove pulls me aside and asks, "When can we leave?"

"In a hurry to get home?"

Her eyes dance. "I hid something in the woods. Maurice thinks he's going to find it first, but my money's on you."

Chasing Dove in the woods has become one of our favorite bedtime sports. My cock throbs in my pants at the thought of a chase to bring in the new year.

My lips brush against hers. "Does this hidden surprise have anything to do with your visit to the doctor?"

I have my suspicious about my fiancée and the slight changes happening to her luscious body, and I am so fucking excited.

"Only one way to find out." She takes a step away from me. "And the winner will be thrilled with his prize."

Henri and Maurice wait for us at the door. I bite back a smile as I follow Dove outside, where it's snowing.

I never believed in fairytales, but in this moment, I know

they exist. I was the Beast. A man so cruel that no one could love me. But then this little bird entered my life, showing me things I never knew were possible. Not only that, but she loved my cousins as well. We are all better men because of her, and I can't wait until she bears our last name. If my suspicions are right, she'll be bearing our children soon, too. Our family is safe and full of love. The best ending to any fairytale if you ask me.

To discover the rest of Sarah's backlist, please visit her website at:

www.SarahBale.com

## ABOUT THE AUTHOR

Sarah Bale's family always knew she was destined to write romances when they saw the elaborate stories she created for her Barbie dolls. At fifteen she penned her first book, which will never see the light of day if she has any say.

When Sarah isn't writing, she enjoys spending time with her family and friends, and also planning what she'd do in a zombie apocalypse. One of her favorite pastimes is attending comic cons, where she can nerd out over all things Marvel. She is a USA Today Bestselling Author living in Oklahoma and doesn't plan on leaving anytime soon.

Made in the USA
Columbia, SC
26 September 2022